MY TEARS AND WORDS

ILLUMINATING THE PATH TO HEALING

K GOPICHAND

Made with ♥ on the Notion Press Platform
www.notionpress.com

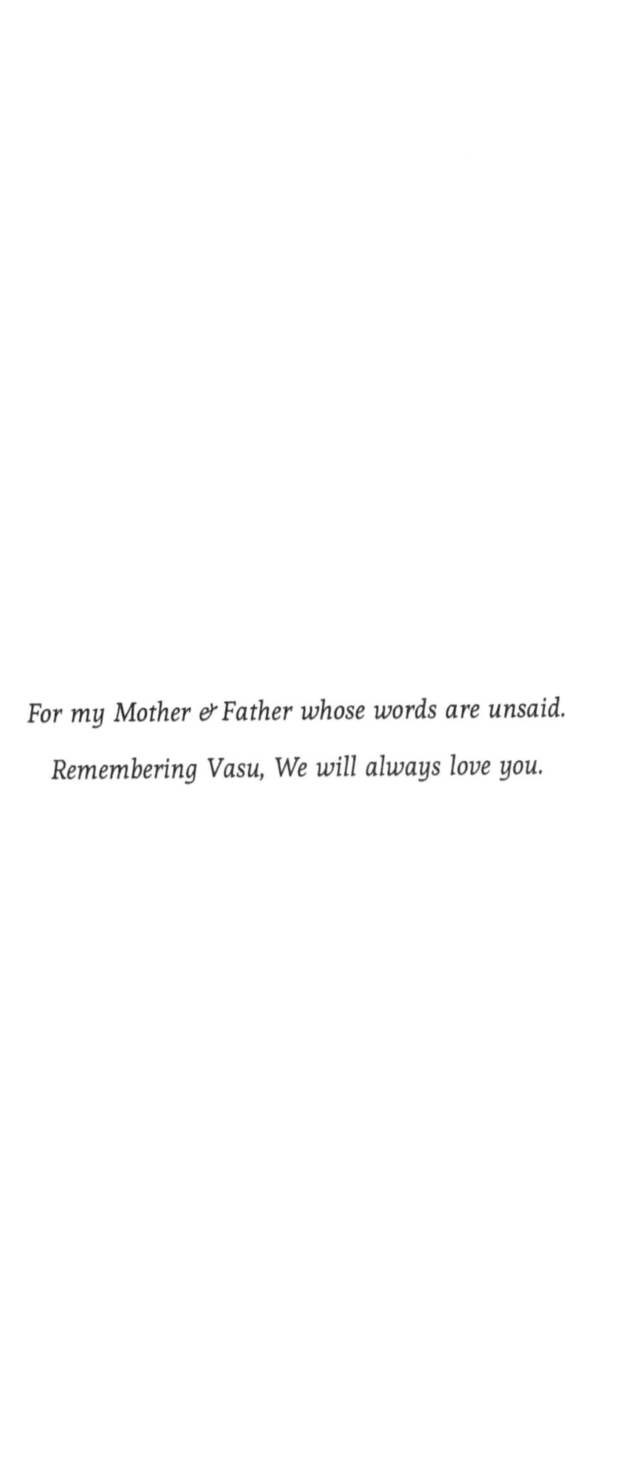

For my Mother & Father whose words are unsaid.

Remembering Vasu, We will always love you.

Contents

Acknowledgements

I extend my heartfelt gratitude to my parents, Ravi and Jayanthi, whose unwavering guidance and invaluable life lessons have shaped me into the person I am today.Without their love and wisdom, this book would not have been possible. I also want to thank my sister, Charishma, for her constant support and encouragement.

To my dearest friends, Roopesh,SaiKumar,Mahesh and Vamsidhar, your encouragement and support have been my pillars of strength throughout this journey. Roopesh,SaiKumar and Mahesh for your daily conversations that inspire me, and Vamsidhar, for your unwavering belief in my endeavors, even from afar.

I owe a debt of gratitude to myself for embarking on this writing journey. Despite uncertainties about its reception, I persevered, driven by the hope that my words would resonate with others.A special thanks to Archana Balasubramaniam,whose unwavering cheer and belief in my abilities have fueled my determination to see this project through.

To all those who have played a part, whether big or small, in bringing this book to fruition, I am immensely grateful. Your support has been the wind beneath my wings.

Faces Of The Story

- Krish
- Anshu (Krish's Girlfriend)
- Subinay (Krish's Friend)
- Vaishnavi (Krish's Friend)
- Vyas (Krish's Father)
- Jayanthi (Krish's Mother)
- Chitra (Krish's Sister)
- Deva (Vaishnavi's Father)
- Mrs.Deva (Vaishnavi's Mother)
- Uncle (Krish's Uncle / Jayanthi's Brother)

Prologue

Krish.

I treaded the familiar path toward Anshu's house, my heart fluttered with a blend of anticipation and trepidation. Each step felt heavier, burdened with the weight of unspoken words.

Today, I would finally lay bare the feelings that had long resided within me, ready to propose to her. When we first met, I wanted to write a poem and propose, but I couldn't. Today, I want to say it and the poem goes like..

Writing about you every night,
is my favorite time,everyday.
Don't know how many times I loved myself every night,
when I think about you everyday.
Blue picture of you in my mind every night,
makes my eyes smile and stops my pen everyday.
The day when blue turns magenta, I looked back and
saw your eyes,
The day your words hit my heart,
The day my hand couldn't stop writing about you,
Was my favorite time,every night and everyday.

What if she didn't feel the same way? What if my feelings were misplaced, a figment of my own longing? But amidst these doubts, a flicker of hope remained, fueled by the countless stolen glances and fleeting smiles we had shared.

I was crossing the road with these thoughts.My heart leaped into my throat as I turned, just in time to see the headlights of an oncoming truck bearing down upon me with terrifying speed.

Time slowed to a crawl as fear gripped me, paralyzing my every muscle. I tried to move, to escape the impending collision, but my limbs refused to obey.

The peaceful evening shattered by screeching tires and blaring horns. In an instant, fate took hold, bending the laws of physics as metal and flesh collided in a chaotic clash.

People around me were running towards me,their voices, a jumbled chorus, echoed through the fog of my pain and confusion.

Everyone was screaming,I'm losing my consciousness and when my eyes were closing,All the moments that happened in my life started to relive.

I lost my consciousness and my memories started playing in my head with my love at first sight,mom.

RELIVING BEGINS

1
Fate Bowls a Curveball

The sun was still hanging in the sky as we walked back home from school, my feet itching to break into a run. Mom was on one side, my sister on the other. Mom held my bag in one hand, while my sister, with her head buried in my mom's phone, was probably lost in whatever world she dives into after school. I kicked a small pebble along the sidewalk, trying to keep it bouncing in front of me.

"I'll get you two some snacks," Mom said as we neared the house.I was barely listening. My mind was already on the cricket game. I knew the guys would be playing by now.

I pushed open the front door and tossed my school bag onto the couch. My eyes immediately found my cricket bat leaning against the wall. I grabbed it and swung it a few times in the air, feeling the weight of it, imagining that perfect shot. My sister plopped down on the couch, still glued to her phone like it was some kind of lifeline.

"I'm going to play cricket with my friends," I called out as I made for the door.

"Mm-hmm," she muttered, not even bothering to look up. I waited for a second, just in case she'd actually acknowledge me. She didn't. Typical. I rolled my eyes, but I didn't let it bother me. There were more important things waiting outside.

I stepped out, feeling the warm breeze hit my face. I could hear the distant shouts and laughter of the other kids. That was my cue. I bolted down the front steps, my sneakers pounding against the pavement as I ran towards the playground where I knew they'd be.

Behind me, the house grew quieter as the door clicked shut. For a moment, I glanced back through the window, catching a glimpse of my sister. She was still on the couch, eyes on her screen. She didn't even know I'd left. Not that it mattered. Out here, under the fading sun, with the sounds of my friends in the air, this was where I wanted to be.

As I made my way down the familiar path to the playground, I could already hear the excited chatter and laughter of my friends echoing through the air. They were warming up for the match, their voices blending with the rhythmic thud of the ball hitting the bat. My steps quickened with anticipation. By the time I reached the field, I was already picturing myself smashing a six over the boundary.

The next hour flew by in a blur of running, shouting, and that pure, unfiltered joy of the game. We played like there was nothing else in the world, our energy bouncing off each other, the sun slowly dipping lower in the sky. The field was alive with every swing of the bat, every cheer, and every competitive shout.

But as the sky began to change, the golden light melting into deeper shades of purple and blue, I knew our time was almost up. The streetlights flickered on one by one, casting long, stretching shadows on the ground. We stretched out those final minutes, reluctant to let go, but eventually, the darkening sky signaled the end of the game.

Breathless and satisfied, I dusted off my pants and started the slow walk back home. My heart was still pounding, a mix of the adrenaline from the game and the quiet peace that comes at the end of a good day. As I walked, I could still hear the laughter of my friends fading behind me, and for a moment, the world felt perfectly right.

I stepped through the front door, and the scent of old wood and warm spices greeted me. The dim light in the hallway flickered, casting long shadows that danced against the walls. Something felt off. Mom and Chitra were silent. I paused, listening. The usual hum of the fridge was absent, and the ticking of the wall clock seemed louder, more insistent, like a heartbeat in the quiet.

A sudden gust of wind rushed through the open doorway, catching my breath. The door behind me slammed shut with a deafening thud, the sound echoing through the empty rooms. My heart leapt. I spun around, my pulse quickening, as the hairs on my arms stood on end. The familiar comfort of home now felt strange, unsettling. The silence thickened, wrapping around me.

I stood still, straining to hear anything—a creak, a whisper, something to break the tension. But nothing came, just the steady drumming of rain against the windows. Minutes ticked by like hours. Eventually, the front door creaked open, and my father's heavy footsteps echoed in the hallway, grounding me in the reality of his presence.

Sensing my presence, he looked up, his eyes meeting mine with a mixture of sadness and resolve. "Hey, Dad, what's going on?" I asked, my voice barely cutting through the thick air between us. My words hung there, unanswered, as he took a deep breath, his gaze dropping for a moment as if searching for the right words in the floor.

He sighed heavily, patting the space beside him on the couch, indicating for me to sit down. "Son, I need to talk to you about something important" he began, his tone serious.

"Tomorrow is going to be a big day for us," he continued, his gaze steady. "It's going to be the last day you'll see this city and your friends. We're shifting to another place."

"Okay, Dad," I replied, feeling blank and lost. It was as if my mind had gone blank, unable to comprehend what he had just said. Moving? Leaving everything behind? It hit me like a sudden wave, leaving me speechless and unsure of what to think or feel.

Mom's voice rang out from the living room, sharp with urgency. "Why are you telling him like that?" she exclaimed, her tone laced with frustration. "He's just a 13-year-old kid!"

Dad's calm voice interjected, breaking the tension. "I know that, honey. Don't shout," he said reassuringly, his tone soothing. "He's getting scared."

Dad's hand gently ruffled my hair, "You'll study hard wherever you are, right?" he asked, his eyes searching mine for confirmation.

"Yes, Dad," I replied.

The next day, I went to my friend's home and broke the news that we were leaving the city. He fell silent for a moment, processing the sudden revelation, but all he managed to say was a simple 'okay'.

We spent some time watching cartoons together, the weight of impending departure hanging in the air. Before leaving, I made sure to say goodbye to his mom.

"Why are you lingering at his place for so long? What's going on there?"Chitra asked.

"Nothing.I told him that we are leaving today", I replied.

Dad said from the hall "Son, stay in your uncle's home for two days, i will come and pick you once we shift everything"

"Dad, but I will get bored there,"I ignored him. Your cousins will be there, dad replied.

My uncle came and took me to his home. I spent the day playing and watching TV with my cousins, but soon enough, boredom set in. Feeling overwhelmed by homesickness, I couldn't hold back the tears. Sensing my distress, my uncle dialed my mom's number and handed me the phone. "He's crying," he explained to her. With a comforting tone, Mom assured him, "His dad will come this evening."

Dad came that day night. "What happened, son? Why are you crying?" Dad's concerned voice broke through my tears as he entered my uncle's house.

"Dad, I'll come with you. I can't stay here alone without Mom," I choked out between sobs. "Okay, I came to take you with me. Let's go,"Dad replied, his reassurance instantly lifting my spirits.I was so happy and he told me to wait outside.

"Take care of him," Uncle said. Grandma called my dad and said, "He can't live without his mother, he's just a kid, you know"

"Yeah," Dad nodded, glancing at me before turning to Grandma. "Take care of your health," he assured her.

"I know the person who is leaving his own town will be a broken person," Uncle said.

Dad smiled warmly and replied "Take care".

"Son, Are you okay with moving from this town?" Dad asked.

"Yes dad,"I replied.We drove for 3 hours on the bike and we reached the new home and town.Mom cleared her throat "Welcome home Krish" I ran to her and said "this home is so good".Chitra hit me on my back "There is a ground near the home"

"I need many friends too," I said.I went to the ground along with my dad and saw a few people playing cricket.I don't know why but i loved that sport.

"Tomorrow you will go to your new school, son,"dad informed me.

"Okay dad"

From the kitchen, Mom's voice interrupted our conversation. "Let's have dinner," she called out.

As Dad and Chitra sat down at the dining hall to eat, I heard Mom's voice calling me from outside. "We're eating at the outside stairs, I'll feed you."

Maa,I will go to play cricket after school, I said."You can, don't need to ask me Krish"

I am so excited for the next day.By thinking about the day, I slept with joy.

The first day at my new school was amazing. I met someone new named Subinay. We hit it off right away and talked a lot. Thanks to him, I quickly felt at home in the school.

After school, I rushed to join the new guys for a game of cricket. Time flew by, and before I knew it, it was getting dark.When I finally got home, I was met by my mom's gentle voice. "Krish, you need to sleep now," she said with a smile. "Go and sleep in that room."

Tired but still buzzing with excitement from the game, I obeyed my mom and headed to bed.

I heard dad was shouting in the middle of the night.I woke up and went to the hall room.Chitra held my hand "It's nothing, go and sleep".I went with her and slept.

"Krish,You need to go",the voice echoed in my dream and that woke me up.

Dad looked up from the newspaper. "You're up early, son. Planning to play in the morning too?"

"No, Dad, I just had a bad dream," I replied, taking the newspaper and pretending to read it.

My dad smiled and playfully tapped me on the head. "Dad, I was actually reading," I protested with a laugh.

Going to school was a burden for me until I made some friends.We used to play during breaks and we do the homeworks of afternoon classes at lunch.In the evening, the playground is my home.

After a few months, I woke up to the sound of my dad shouting at my mom again in the middle of the night. This time, my sister Chitra was crying as she watched them argue. I didn't understand what was happening.

I stood silently by the door, watching as Dad argued with Mom. "It wasn't my fault," he insisted.

"You just don't know how to live! All you do is write that damn book!" Mom yelled, filled with frustration. Chitra stepped in, trying to calm Mom down.

I followed Dad into the hallway. "Why are you both fighting, Dad?"I asked softly.

"It's nothing, son," he replied."You trust me, right? Go and get some sleep. You have school tomorrow."

Early in the morning, I noticed that Mom was unusually quiet. There was no smile on her face, and her silence weighed heavily on me.I don't know what's happening at home,but it troubled me deeply,

"You peed your pants,"Subinay asked.

"What?No,"I replied.

"Then why is your face like that?"Subinay questioned. "I'm fine" I answered, trying to brush off the embarrassment and change the subject.

Mom and Dad were back to being good to each other, but I still couldn't figure out why they fought sometimes. Despite that, my 7th and 8th grades were great, especially because I got to play cricket every day.

When I asked Dad to buy me a cricket kit, he shook his head and said, "Focus on your studies, son."

"Dad, I really need it,"I persisted, hoping he would understand how much cricket meant to me.

"I said no!" Dad shouted. "You play enough after school every day. Just focus on your studies."

"But Dad, I want to join the coaching center," I pleaded.

"Will you stop arguing with me? I said no, and it's final," Dad retorted firmly.

"I am not arguing dad,"I replied.

After that conversation with my father, I fell silent. That night, I stayed at Subinay's home and poured out everything that had happened. It felt good to confide in him. The next morning, I returned home early,

"Dad just ignored me," I muttered to myself as I prepared to leave for school. "I'm going to school, Bye, Mom."

"Krish, you still have more time,"Mom said with her soft voice."I'll join up with Subinay," I replied, trying to hide the disappointment in my voice.

"Tomorrow our friends are joining the coaching center," Subinay said.Everyone in the class,talking about that. "I need to talk to my parents about it, Subinay," I replied.

I walked up to my dad and mustered up the courage to say, "I'm joining the coaching center tomorrow."

"You've started again, huh?" Dad replied, his tone stern.

"Dad, please," I requested.

"Son, listen to your father," Mom said.

"Mom, you too?" I questioned, feeling a sense of disappointment."Maa, I love to play cricket," I pleaded, hoping she would support me.

"I know, we know it, but your studies are important," Mom said gently, her voice edged with concern. "Mom, but I never said I won't study. Please, Mom," I pleaded, trying to convey my willingness to balance both cricket and studies."We can't make it, just keep it as a hobby," Mom replied, her words weighing heavily on my heart. Chitra watched silently as the conversation unfolded. Without saying a word to them, I left home.

As I walked for an hour, all I could think about was my parents decision. "They care for me, so why are they stopping me?"

When I returned home, the atmosphere was tense, and Chitra was in tears. They had been searching for me, and Dad had gone out to find me. "Where have you been?" Mom asked, her voice filled with anger.

"None of your business. It's my life. Of course you don't care," I replied, my eyes dim with hot tears and frustration. Dad arrived and heard my words before silently heading to his room.

The next day, when Subinay brought up the topic of joining the coaching center, I hesitated and finally admitted that I wasn't going to join. He quickly changed the subject to WWE, diverting our conversation away from the topic of cricket.

Still not feeling quite like myself, I started coming home late on purpose for a few days. Subinay was supportive, so I'd hang out at his place after school.

I used to take walks in the evening. So, as usual, I was walking, lost in my thoughts, everything around me a blur.

"Krish, it's too late. Come eat dinner," Mom called out. "I ate outside with Subinay,"I replied.Chitra came over to talk to me.

"Why are you giving them a hard time , Krish?" she uttered.

"Are you mad? That's the question you need to ask them.I am already having a hard time.Please Chitra, I thought you understood me"I said firmly.

"Of course,I did," Chitra replied.

"No,I'm not seeing that.Can you leave me alone for a moment, I shouted".She left without saying a word.

Since that day, I don't know why, I didn't feel like talking to anyone.That's how the 7th standard ended in school.I used to spend most of my holidays playing cricket.All summer holidays together, I didn't even speak 10 sentences to my dad.

My first day of 9th standard,I was walking through the school.

"Hey Krish, can you spare me a few minutes, please?" the Principal called out. Little did I know, that moment would change my life. "Yes, ma'am, of course," I replied.

"She's Vaishnavi, a new student joining your 9th-grade class. Could you please show her the classroom?" the Principal requested.

"Sure, I'll take care of her," I replied. Leading the path, I took the lead as we climbed the stairs together.

"What's your name,"she whispered.

"Why? Didn't you hear when the principal called me?"I asked, a bit annoyed."And why are you whispering?"

"Eww,Okay kid. I am Vaishnavi.Keep your cool,"she replied.

"Kid?Be careful with your words and I didn't ask your name," I said with arrogance.

"Okay, Okay sorry," she apologized.

I shouted at her but when she whispered and asked my name,I got a smile on my face after so many days.

"Can you just follow me please?" I requested.

"Okay,sorry again,"she said.

I laughed instantly after that and she saw it. "Wow,This kiddo has a smile," she teased.

"If you dare call me that again, you'll regret it," I said sternly. "Now that we're here, keep quiet and go inside," I directed, pointing towards the classroom door.

After school I told Subinay about her.He said he knew her and she lives on our street as well.

"What? I've never seen her," I said, surprised. "They must be new here," Subinay replied.I thought of talking with her again.I know I am arrogant and that's what holds me back from talking to people.How can I spread joy when I'm not feeling it myself?

Subinay asked, "You wanna talk to her, don't you?"

"No, Subinay, I don't want to talk to anyone. I've just been arrogant with everyone. Just leave me be like this," I replied.

"How much longer will you stay like this?"He raised his voice.

"Why are you shouting, Subinay?" I asked, hoping to calm him down.

"Krish, when you're going through a tough time and pushing everyone away, remember that you might be distancing yourself from the one who can help you heal too," Subinay said.

Subinay's words took me by surprise. I didn't understand where they came from, but they hit me hard. It felt like he knew something I didn't want to admit. Even though I always tried to seem tough, what he said made me wonder if pushing everyone away was the right thing to do. Maybe, in trying to be the best, I forgot how important it is to let others help me through tough times.

I hate myself when I smile.Even if I smile, I immediately remember the fight with my dad and every time it is remembered, the laughter stops and the eyes get dim.

I was playing in the ground, lost in these thoughts. Suddenly, Chitra came down and told me there was a visitor at home, specifically for me.

As I climbed the stairs, I overheard someone's voice saying, "No, from Bangalore, Mrs.Vyas," It sounded familiar. "We shifted recently"

"It's Vaishnavi,"I called Chitra over and asked, "What is she doing here?"

"Vaishnavi said she needs to talk to you," Chitra replied. "There's nothing to talk about with her," I murmured under my breath.

Holding Vaishnavi's hand, I said, "That's enough with my mom. Let's talk outside."

"Okay, Mrs. Vyas. I'll talk to him and come again," Vaishnavi said before leaving.

I looked at her angrily for a while. "What's there to talk about with me, huh?"

"About school, kiddo. I'm new here," Vaishnavi replied calmly.

"I said don't call me like that. Can't you understand?There's nothing to talk about school. Just come and go daily," I replied curtly.

She said,"Look at you, I don't think you're as angry inside as you appear. I don't know what you're thinking, but can't you come out of it?"

"I'm fine, and I don't care about your thoughts. Understand? If you're done, please leave," I requested firmly.Vaishnavi left after that. With tears in her eyes, Mom uttered, "Why are you being like that? You have changed, Krish."

"Mom, your tears mean nothing to me; they won't change a thing. I cried more than you, and that's why I'm dry-eyed even when you shed tears,"I said, feeling my heart sink.I left to go to the playground, needing some time alone.

I was sitting on the bench in the playground.Vaishnavi overheard the conversation from the stairs and silently made her way to where I sat.She sat next to me. "I'm not in a good mood right now. Please don't try to irritate me," I said. "I won't say anything," she replied softly. We sat in silence, the evening slowly turning into night.

"Okay, go home, Vaishnavi. It's already 6:30," I conveyed gently, afraid of losing my temper with her.

"Not just for me, but for you too," she replied.

I tried to hold back the tears in my eyes. "I'm not myself," I admitted. She listened quietly and then said, "You can talk to me."

I stopped myself from sharing with her. It was the worst feeling I've ever experienced. I wanted to be alone but also longed for someone to talk to. We sat there for an hour in silence.

"Vaishnavi, it's getting late. Should we head home?" I asked, ready to leave the playground."You can call me 'Vaishu'," she said, and that's when our eyes met. I didn't reply,I just looked into her eyes.

"Let's go," I said, and as we walked home, I noticed Vaishnavi's expression, as if she felt I was being cold to her."Krish, do you enjoy walking?" Vaishnavi questioned, breaking the silence between us.

"I used to walk whenever I felt low. Why?" I responded, curious about her question.

"Really? Me too. But not necessarily when I feel low. I just enjoy walking and thinking about things," she replied, sharing a bit about herself.

"Great! And?" I responded,interested in hearing more about her. "Hmmmm... I read books, and I like to write down thoughts about someone or maybe quotes," she replied, sharing another aspect of her interests.

"My father loves words. What do you think makes them so special?" I asked, seeking her insight."I don't know but it is like evolving to me,"She replied.

She really loves books.I can see that in her face.I thought to myself that I enjoyed her company.

"Krish, whenever you feel low, you can talk to me. You know where my home is, right?" Vaishnavi remarked.

"Yes,I do,"I replied.

"Okay, see you tomorrow," she waved as I reached my home, ending our conversation for the day.

I went home, where Dad was waiting for me. "Please be calm," Mom said in a low voice."What did you say to your mom?" Dad shouted as soon as I entered.

"I just told the truth, Dad. I'll say it again. Listen carefully. You really don't care about me. I can see that. You know what you did, and you also know why I am like this. I'm not mad. I really hate my life. Every time I see my face in the mirror, I literally hate myself. I loved that sport, and that's all I know," I said, pouring out my emotions.

"Okay, you can think that I'm not perfect in this sport and that I just have an attraction to it," I accepted, understanding his perspective.

"Can you lower your voice?"Dad said,arguing for calmness.

"Let me speak, Dad. You can think that I just have an attraction to it, but I didn't even try, Dad. I didn't even try. I lost. I lost without even starting, Dad," I replied, tears welling up in my eyes.

"Krish, stop crying," Mom said, her own eyes wet with tears. "This is not the only day that I'm crying, Mom,"I replied, my voice trembling with my crying.

Dad didn't utter a single word.He wordlessly headed to his room.I am just seeing him "All you do is that,just hiding in your face and writing your diary", I said aloud.

I went to the balcony and sat on the stairs.Chitra was there waiting for me "What's all this Krish?"

"What?"

"He is our dad, is that how you talk to him?"She said, her tone concerned. "I know, Chitra. I don't want to hate them either. I hate that I hate them. I just can't come out of it," I replied.

There was a strange silence when I woke up in the morning. Subinay arrived home at school time and noticed something amiss with my parents. "Bro, is everything okay?" he asked.

"Nothing happened. Let's go," I replied. Going to school makes me feel better somehow. It's like my escape room. So I never miss any class.Subinay is aware of that; he makes sure I'm at school every day.

We were at the ground since the class had not yet started. Vaishnavi waved at me, and I simply nodded my head.

"What have you two done now?" Subinay asked sarcastically. "What did we do?" I replied, puzzled by his question.

"Bro, she waved at you."

"Yeah."

"And you nodded."

"Yeah."

"Yeah?,OMG.That will not happen with you,"Subinay said.

"Chill Subinay.We met yesterday and talked for a while.We were at the playground all evening,"I explained.

"Really,Then,why are you just nodding?.Let me call her,"Subinay said. "No,no wait.Why do you do that?" I tried to stop him.

"Hey Vaishnavi, Krish is calling you!" Subinay shouted across the ground.She noticed us. "Coming, Krish," she called out. My heart started pounding. I had met her yesterday, but I don't know.

"Okay, Subinay, he called me, so you can leave," Vaishnavi replied.

"Oh, okay okay.I will leave.Talk with him",Subinay said. "Why are you asking him to leave?"I questioned.

"Kiddo,Keep your cool.Can we go to class?",Vaishnavi said.For a time, I felt like I was facing empty spaces, even though I was surrounded by thousands. But Vaishnavi filled that void in no time. I never tried to find a reason why I liked her. The only thing I thought was that I enjoyed her company.

"Okay, take your bags and let's move," I replied. We went to class together and had a really good day.

I was at the playground again after school, waiting for her. It was already 6 p.m., and she still hadn't shown up.

'**Krish, you can talk to me**,' her words were running through my head.I thought if she comes today, I will tell her everything.

"Hey Kiddo".My heart started pounding again when I heard that voice.

"You are waiting for me,right?"Vaishnavi asked.

"Why would I wait for you?I'm just sitting here. I'll be here every day." I had hinted to her that I would be there daily in the evenings.

She showed me her mobile "I will write everything in it,"she said.

"You write what?"I questioned.

"Everything Krish.I write about mom,dad,you and school.Everything.Books are..."

"Okay, okay. Let's stop talking about books and all, please," I replied.

She laughed. "Okay, I won't. Relax," she reassured me. She was only here for 5 minutes, but I could see my happiness reflected in her eyes. Whenever I smile, Vaishu's eyes seem to shine even brighter. It's true that our happiness also lives in someone's eyes.

She ignored my response and continued, "Let me ask you a serious question, Krish. What is life?"

"Stop it, yaar," I protested. "I said no to books and words (quotes). You're asking about this again."She didn't give up until I gave her an answer.

"Hey, answer it, nah," she insisted, nudging me on my shoulder. "It's not about books, Krish."

"Ouch, wait. Why are you hitting me? Hold on," I said angrily, rubbing my shoulder."You need to tell it fast. This is not an exam, Krish. You are really a kid," she teased, a playful smile on her lips. "Come again" I said.

"Okay, okay.Sorry, answer to that" She asked.

"Maybe moments",I replied.

"Good answer, Krish. Can we go to my home?" she asked. I hesitated, but she insisted, eventually convincing me to accompany her. "My mom will be happy if she sees you,"She said.

"Ahh,Your mom knows me?"I queried.

We were walking to her place "Of course she knew you Krish".I couldn't help but wonder what she had told her mom. "Don't worry,I said good things about you,"she said.

Walking with her felt different. Forgetting everything else, I just wanted to walk with her.I was watching her eyes, and she said, "What? Why are you looking like that?"

"Good things about me? Wanna hear that," I replied. She was silent for a while and then caught my eye. "You're nervous," she observed.

"I am nervous..no"I shook my head.I was nervous, but I didn't say it.We reached her place.Vaishnavi mom was outside and waiting for her "Where have you been,Vaishu?"

"You can see that,mom,"she pointed at me.I lifted my head and greeted her, "Hello, Mrs. Deva. I am Krish."She walked towards me, saying, "I know you. She always talks about you. Come inside."

We went inside. The house was filled with art. Standing in the doorway, I asked, "Vaishnavi, you never said that you like art."

"Haha.My dad loves art,"Vaishnavi replied.Vaishnavi and her mother talked with me for an hour. I felt so good. "I have to go, Vaishnavi. It's late," I said, realizing the time.

Vaishnavi came up to the doorstep with me. I whispered, "Your mom knows everything about me." She laughed and replied, "If I know you, the world will know you, but they don't know who you are."

I reached home,thinking about her. I had enjoyed every moment of my day, but as I was about to sleep, the only thing that hurt me was that I had left cricket behind.

When we truly love something and we know we won't have it anymore, crying for a day and talking with someone won't heal the pain. It's a wound that will hurt until the end.

All your loved ones can do is help you write a new story where the happiness outweighs the hurt. They'll help you carry the bag filled with sadness.Like I found my happiness,Vaishnavi doesn't know what I'm having in my bag but she is helping me to carry it.

I fell asleep thinking of her,but in the middle of the night,I heard Mom and dad fighting again.

"You always say that reason,I don't care,"Mom shouted.This time,Chitra was sleeping.I was there and I didn't go to them.I closed my eyes like I don't care.

"Try to understand me,"Dad said slowly, but I had already drifted off to sleep. I found myself dreaming the same dream again. "Krish, you need to go," played in my mind.

The next morning, Subinay and I sat silently in school. Vaishnavi was late that day. "What happened to you both?" she asked, noticing our unusual silence.

"Krish's parents fought yesterday, and he doesn't know why. His mind is just messed up," Subinay replied to Vaishnavi. I just wanted to know why they were fighting suddenly. She looked at me "Kiddo,We will talk about it but for now we need to go to the class."

Subinay picked my bag "Yes,let's do it dude".Vaishnavi was checking on me in every class leisure time.I never listen to the classes when something happens at home.

The last class started, and Vaishnavi threw a paper at me. It read, "Wait for me after the class." I nodded, and I waited at the school gate with Subinay. Vaishnavi joined us and said, "Krish, we need to talk."

"Okay, I understand. You both are keeping me aside," he said, showing a hint of possessiveness.

"Krish, can you meet me today at my home?" Vaishnavi asked. Despite knowing she wanted to console me, I decided not to go. The thought of discussing everything in front of her mom made me hesitant.

"Krish, say something," Vaishnavi urged. I didn't reply, lost in my thoughts. "Hey kiddo, you're here?" she called out again.

This time, she was right. I was thinking about the consequences like a kid. "I'm not sure, and I'll try to come," I replied hesitantly. She shouted at me, "Try? Just come. You'll stay at the playground alone instead of coming to my home."

"Okay. I will,"I said.

I reached home and stayed in. I decided not to go to the ground or to Vaishnavi's home either. Lying on the bed, I stared at the wall. If I didn't visit her, she would come to find me at the playground. So, I stayed.

"Are you not going to the playground?" Chitra questioned. I replied with a simple "No."

"I think Vaishnavi is waiting for you, Krish," Chitra said, expressing her concern.

"How did you know?"I asked.

"She's in the hall room with Mom," Chitra replied. I made my way to the hall room and asked, "Vaishnavi, can we go?"Once we stepped outside, I questioned her, "Why did you come here?"

"You said that you would come, but you didn't," she said.

"So what Vaishnavi?"I said aloud.

"Krish, calm down," she said soothingly. "I thought you forgot, and I searched for you in the playground. You were not there. I wished that we would meet today."

"Please Krish."

She held my hand, and we walked to her home hand in hand. "Mom, Krish is here,"she announced as we entered.Her mom glanced at us and said, "Come inside. I will make tea for you both."

"Mom, not here. We should head to the terrace," Vaishnavi insisted. "Why the terrace?" I questioned. Her mom gave the green light without a second thought.

"Krish, there's no need to fret. Follow me," Vaishnavi calmly said. We headed to the terrace, where a few chairs were arranged. "Sit on these,"Vaishnavi said, pointing to the lounge chairs.

"What on earth are we doing here Vaishnavi?"I questioned.

"Look at the sky, Krish. You know, whenever I fight with my mom and dad, I just come here to look at the sky. Believe me, it gives a good vibe. I'm not saying it makes you happy, but it helps to heal. It has a healing effect," Vaishnavi said.

"What is this Vaish....."I tried to stop her from doing all this."Don't talk,Just look at the sky,"she said to my eyes.

I started looking at the sky, expecting her to console me or advise me to talk to my parents. However, all she said was to look at the sky. Time passed, and we were still looking at the sky in silence.

A few minutes later, the weight of the recent events flooded my mind.The fight with my parents and my own arrogance played over and over in my mind. My eyes conveyed that it couldn't bear to see it all, urging me to close them. So, I closed my eyes.But my heart protested, insisting that it couldn't contain all the pain inside. It urged me to open my eyes. My eyes couldn't handle it all, so I stopped looking into the sky and instead they welled up with tears.

I wiped away my tears, continuing to gaze at the sky. The surroundings embraced a profound calmness. All that met my eyes was the moon. For the first time in a while, I found solace, and the world felt undeniably beautiful.

I looked at Vaishnavi, and she was sleeping. In that moment, my heart pleasantly whispered, "She helped you to hold your pain." My eyes formed a smile while tears streamed down my face.That day, I learned the profound value held in two simple yet powerful words: the smile that she brought to my face and the tears of happiness that followed.

2

Bonds Beyond Books

With the final exams of our 9th standard announced to begin in 20 days, Vaishnavi, Subinay, and I found ourselves at a crossroads.The weight of impending exams loomed large, and the pressure to perform well intensified with each passing day. Determined not to face this challenge alone, Subinay and Vaishnavi made a pact—a pact to tackle this hurdle together.

I held his neck tight, my fingers digging into the soft flesh of his throat. The pulse beneath my grip was frantic, mirroring the fear in his wide eyes."Whose plan is it?" I asked, my voice cold and demanding.

Subinay struggled, his hands clawing at mine in a futile attempt to free himself. His breath came in ragged gasps, and his face was turning a shade of red that bordered on purple. "Leave me, Krish. I'll tell you. Just let go!" he screamed, his voice cracking and filled with desperation.They always try to do something to stick with me, hoping to sway my moods.

"Hey, come back here!" I shouted, a grin spreading across my face. I took off after him, my sneakers pounding against the pavement.Our friends watched and cheered, turning our chase into an impromptu spectacle.

As I closed the gap between us, I reached out and grabbed the back of his shirt. He twisted around, and we both tumbled to the ground in a tangle of limbs and laughter.We rolled over each other and wrestled playfully.

This was so usual for us to fight in the playground.They know we are having fun.From a distance, it might have looked like we were serious, but everyone knew we were just having fun.Then Vaishnavi showed up.

"Guys,"she laughs.

After our little fight, we decided to take a break and relax on the benches.Vaishnavi was still laughing. "It's not a fight, only one guy was hitting. That's not called a fight,"

Subinay was staring at her and said "I spared him a hit because he's my friend."

"Poor Subinay,"She laughed hard.

Subinay stood up quickly "Okay whatever.We are studying together.Before that,Vaishnavi needs to do one thing."

"What?"Vaishnavi asked.

"You need to stop laughing,"Subinay replied.

He was so frustrated, and we finally stopped making fun of him. I agreed to study together for our exams, and Vaishnavi suggested that we would start from the next day.

Vaishnavi proposed, "Let's prepare for the first exam at my place." Subinay and I agreed to that.

"Perfect,"Vaishnavi was excited.I thought it would help me to prepare for my exams well.I got less marks last year after I stopped playing cricket.We chatted the entire way back to our respective homes, teasing Subinay along the way.

I went to the terrace to follow the thing that Vaishnavi showed me–looking at the sky.This time the sky showed me the funny evening that I had today.It evoked the feeling of someone saying "Krish, the laughter you expressed today was from the soul."

I sat on the wall, gazing at the sky before eventually heading to my room to sleep. My parents always sleep in the hall room, while Chitra sleeps on the bedroom floor. I sleep on the bed.

That night, I had a dream. I was playing cricket, and my dad was cheering me on from the sidelines.A few years ago, I dreamt the same dream; Once a fleeting daydream,, it has now metamorphosed into a haunting nightmare.

The same dream inspired me and it breaks my heart too.I was awake that night,not asleep.

The alarm rings "You are awake already",Chitra asked.She thought I was going to the ground again.Chitra loved to see if I start playing cricket again.I stopped playing cricket in the mornings.

"No Chitra,just trouble sleeping,"I replied.I told Chitra that I would study at Vaishnavi's house today.I asked her to inform mom and dad.

Subinay and I waited for Vaishnavi. We had formed a routine of going to school together and returning home together.

"Today we're studying," Vaishnavi said cheerfully. It felt different going to her house instead of the playground, where I usually go to be alone.

"At 6, I'll be leaving my place and picking up Krish," Subinay mentioned.The class started.In the middle of the class,Subinay choked out "You are fine with it,right?"

"You are asking now?"I lowered my voice and said "We were in math class, and the teacher was strict about not chatting."

At the break time I asked Subinay "You can ask me now,Not in her class".

"Okay,"he chuckles.

"Tell me now,why did you ask me that all of a sudden",I asked.He was thinking to say "Krish, I am sorry for putting you in that situation. I believed being with us would make you happy," he expressed.

"Haha,I am grateful you did that Subinay.Thank you.Definitely that will make me happy,"I replied.

"Really?"He was surprised.

"Yes,Subinay."

Subinay feared me, not because of my arrogance. Once he said, "You might seem calm after being arrogant, but I'm scared of how much you must hurt during your tough times, Krish."

Vaishnavi reminded us to meet after school. As Subinay had mentioned, he arrived at my home at 6. Mom was about to ask where I was headed. I looked at Chitra, she told mom "They're going to study together at Vaishnavi's house, Mom."

"Come home before dinner time Krish",mom said.

I left without saying a word to my mom.Subinay was seeing all those "Krish,Come on,reply to her".

"Can we go?" I acted like I didn't hear.

"Bye Mrs.Vyas,"Subinay waved.We went to Vaishnavi's house.Her father was there.He invited us in. "Welcome, boys," Vaishnavi's father greeted us warmly. "Let's put those books away for now. So, which one of you is Krish, and who's Subinay?" he asked with a friendly smile.

Subinay introduced himself and I replied "Hi Mr.Deva,I am Krish."

As Vaishnavi and her mom prepared tea, Subinay observed the artwork in the house. He turned to Vaishnavi's father and said, "Mr.Deva, I can tell you love art. These pieces are incredible."

Mr.Deva laughed.

"Who's your favorite?"Subinay asked him.

He replied "I don't have any favorite artist but I personally love Vincent Van Gogh."We don't know who Vincent was.

"Dad,not now,"Vaishnavi shouts from Kitchen."Okay Vaishu,You love Vincent too,"Mr.Deva said.

Mrs.Deva bought tea for us and said "They both love Vincent."Subinay and I were looking at each other.Vaishnavi was staring at me when he mentioned that artist.

"What?"I whispered.She sat right behind me.

"Nothing,"She whispered back.

"It's okay guys,stop looking at each other.If he starts talking about that artist,you can't study today,"Mrs.Deva told us.

We all laughed hard and she cleared the table in the hall room "You guys can study here."

Vaishnavi's parents excused themselves to another room, giving us space to study. Their hospitality made us feel comfortable. We started with mathematics, and although Subinay and Vaishnavi were better at math than I was, they patiently helped me prepare for the exam that day.

I'm exhausted and I reminded Vaishnavi that Mom told us to be at dinner time, and we've had enough preparation today.

"Sorry,I didn't see the time.Okay let's pick up where we left tomorrow,"Vaishnavi replied.

"Mom, they're leaving,"Vaishnavi called out to her parents.They joined us and kindly insisted that we were welcome to visit anytime. We thanked Vaishnavi's mom for the tea. On our way back home, Subinay turned to me and asked, "Can we go to Vaishnavi's house again tomorrow?"

I said "If she's okay,we will."

"Of Course She will,"Subinay replied.

Upon reaching home, I found Dad waiting for me at the balcony. He entered the house as soon as I arrived.

We studied most of the days at her house.One day,when we were going to school, Subinay said he was going to his relatives house and he couldn't come to Vaishnavi's home.

"Okay Krish,My parents will come home late today.Can we study at your house,"Vaishnavi asked me.

Subinay said "No" aloud.

"We can."I replied.

Subinay pulled me aside and asked urgently, "Krish, what are you doing?"

"I know what I'm doing,"I told him.

His brows furrowed further. "Is it okay? It won't be good if she sees the situation in your house, Krish. Can you answer her questions?"

"It's okay,Subinay.Mom knew her,"I said.

But Subinay wasn't convinced, his concern deepening. "I know that. But she doesn't know that you do not talk to them and why," he argued, his voice tinged with frustration.I took a deep breath "Let her know then.What will happen if she knows?"

"Krish?"

I stepped closer "What?She thinks that I am an idiot? I am."

When Vaishnavi caught up to us, I quickly explained, "I was just asking him where he was going without me."We went to my home together and Subinay left too.I called Chitra "Chitra she will stay here and we will prepare for tomorrow's exam".Chitra walked up to Mom and conveyed it.We started our preparation.

An hour later, Vaishnavi took my mom's mobile and called her parents to inquire about their return. Her mom mentioned that they would be back in a few hours.

Chitra bought cookies for us and she said "Dad is coming".Vaishnavi greeted my dad.

"Hello Kiddo,"My dad replied.

Vaishnavi laughs "I will call him by the same name Mr.Vyas."

He chuckled, picked up his book and went out.Vaishnavi called my dad "Mr.Vyas,You write a diary?"

"No dear,I don't write it daily.Just a few moments,"he replied.

"That's awesome,Mr.Vyas."

"Yeah,if you say so.Okay prepare well" dad giggles.Vaishnavi left after a few hours.Mom and dad didn't disturbed us until she left.

Vaishnavi,Subinay and I didn't have much conversation while the exams were going.I used to leave after the exam was completed.

Finally we waited for each other for the last exam.Subinay came out first and we were waiting for Vaishnavi.Subinay said that he wrote only a few answers.

Vaishnavi stepped out after the exam and met us. "Why are you laughing in the exam hall Subinay?"She asked him. "The question paper was really hard,I don't know the answers for most of them",Subinay replied.

I laughed very hard knowing that he was laughing because the question paper was hard.

"So you mean you are laughing instead of crying"Vaishnavi laughs too.After so many days we are going back to our home together.Vaishnavi stopped and said "I am going to my grandma's town for the summer."

I shouted "No"

"What happened Krish?" they questioned.

I forgot to write the question in the last chapter,I replied.I thought Subinay knew why I shouted.I am thinking "It's hard to admit to them but I would miss Vaishnavi."

"Uff,You scared us.That's okay,"Vaishnavi hit on my shoulder.I asked her when she was about to leave.

"Now,after I reach home"she patted my shoulder. All I could think about was returning to my same old life. She kept talking about her grandma's town the entire way, but I remained silent.

Reaching home,Chitra told mom that they declared holidays for summer.I just sat on the chair for an hour.I recalled that Vaishnavi called Mrs.Deva with my mom's phone.

I didn't think anything and I called Mrs.Deva right away.Vaishnavi lifted "Hello,Krish?"

"Vaishnavi,you are at home right?"

She replied "No Krish,I left.I told you that I was going.You forgot already?"

The words 'I was going' hung in the air, and in that moment, I chose to silently listen to her without uttering a single word.

"Hello?Hello?Krish"

I ended the call abruptly, sprinting towards the playground. The words 'I was going' echoed relentlessly in my mind, racing faster than my hurried steps.

I came to the place where I can breathe.I found a peaceful spot and sat on a bench in the playground. I closed my eyes and thought about her. I remembered the night we sat together under the stars.

When it's hard for me to move on.She helped my losing heart.I was looking at the sky alone and my heart silently whispered a wish that she was there.

2

Missing her was a new feeling. Actually she was there.Whether I looked at the sky, sat on a playground bench, or walked the streets,I felt she was always there with me.

As I wandered through the playground, the afternoon sun casting long shadows across the worn grass, I noticed Subinay approaching. His familiar grin preceded him, mischief twinkling in his eyes. "Hey there," he called out, his voice carrying on the warm breeze.

I turned to greet him, a smile tugging at the corners of my lips. "Hey, Subinay," I replied.

His expression turned mischievous as he drew closer, a playful glint dancing in his eyes. "Got your summer homework done yet?" he teased.I rolled my eyes, a laugh bubbling up in my chest. "Summer homework? Who needs that?" I scoffed.

Subinay chuckled, taking a seat beside me on the weathered bench. 'I should've known you'd be here, soaking up in the sun instead of buried in books."

"Haha,here it feels like I can talk to myself,"I replied. "Krish, let's talk about something else, but we can't avoid our mathematics homework," Subinay interjected.

"Vaishnavi and you have been such a support in math.I really miss her. Every time I'm here, she comes to my mind.This place is filled with memories of us ,"I shared.

I brought up Vaishnavi, and Subinay stayed silent for a while. Wanting to understand his thoughts, I asked, "Is there something you'd like to say, Subinay?"

"Krish...."

Subinay

I visited Krish's home a few days ago. I am the one who had shared information about the cricket coaching center with him. Despite knowing him as someone who was always cheerful, witnessing Krish in a state of sadness made me truly understand the meaning of that emotion.

Realizing the need to apologize, I headed to Krish's father. Aware that Krish typically spends his time in the playground, especially on Sundays, I went to their place. Upon arrival, Mr.Vyas greeted me and said "Subinay, Krish is at the playground."

"Mr.Vyas, I need to talk with you",I replied.

"What happened son?"

"I am sorry,"I apologized.

"For?"

I hugged him and cried "I told Krish about the cricket coaching center.All this happened because of me.I am really sorry Uncle.I made a mistake."

He smiles"Subinay,don't cry.It was not you.Look at me son,sit down."He made me sit in the hall room.Chitra bought us tea and biscuits. "Have some tea,Subinay."

"Subinay, it's important for you to realize that Krish has a deep love for cricket. Even if you hadn't mentioned the coaching center to him, he would have eventually expressed his interest in joining. It just happened a bit sooner than expected."

I held my tears "But it was still my mistake."

"Subinay,mistakes can't be rectified by time.You made my son smile when he needed it most,You left traces of laughter in his life that Krish never forgets.That,for me,is more than enough Subinay.Thank You."Mr.Vyas replied.

Krish

A somber silence settled between us, and tears streamed down his face. Offering a comforting gaze, I softly spoke, "It wasn't you, Subinay. Please don't blame yourself."

"I am sorry Krish,"Subinay said, keeping his head down.

"You want me to beat you to death?"I teased.Subinay laughed.He disclosed another detail, stating,"Vaishnavi contacted me after she completed her preparation at your house."

"Why?What did she ask?"

She inquired "Why is Krish always sad?I saw him crying when we were looking at the sky."I told everything to her,Krish.She observed your behavior with your parents.

"Subinay, just go home," I insisted firmly. "Krish, please, just listen to me," he pleaded.

"No, I'm not angry with you. I just need some time alone," I explained as Subinay left. Unsure of how to face Vaishnavi, I trusted that she understood me. She always had. After some quiet time, reflecting on what Subinay said, I felt grateful to have two best friends.

As I arrived home, I found a chaotic scene.Few people were inside,voices were raised, directed at my dad, my mom was in tears. Chitra quickly pulled me away from the hall room, saying, "Stay here."

"Who are they?"I questioned.Chitra's eyes were teared up "Stay here Krish."

"But Chitra,Mom and dad..."

She stopped me from talking.Chitra told "It's okay Krish,Stay here."Those guys were leaving and stared at me and said "Be careful."

My interactions with my parents were strained, but I found myself unable to remain silent when someone raised their voice at them. The hurtful comments brought tears to my mom's eyes, and even the simple request to 'Stay here' caused Chitra's eyes to fill with tears.

Half of my holidays I was haunted by nightmares revolving around just two words "I was going" and "Stay here."

3
Wandering Hearts

"Krish, wake up. Vaishnavi is calling," Chitra's urgent voice pierced through the fog of sleep, snapping me out of my dreams. With a sudden jolt, I sprang up in bed, my heart racing as I fumbled for my phone.

"Hello Vaishnavi," I managed to croak out, my voice thick with sleep and confusion. Through the haze of drowsiness, I struggled to piece together why Vaishnavi would be calling me at this ungodly hour. Has something happened? My mind raced with possibilities, each more ominous than the last.

"Hey Kiddo,are you sleeping at this time?It's 3PM,"She said.

"You are calling me 'kid',even in the call.Okay,I forgive you,"I replied.She said the words I had been waiting for "I am here Krish,Can we meet?"

In that moment, I found myself in a place where the rest of the world seemed to fade away. I quickly informed Chitra and rushed over to Vaishnavi's house, where she was patiently waiting for me outside my home.

"Why are you running, Krish?"Vaishnavi asked, halting me in my tracks.My eyes met hers, and I greeted her with a simple "Hi"

"Hi?" She said.I stammered, caught off guard by her question. "Um... I... I was..." I struggled to find the words to explain myself.I found myself just staring at her.

"Krish, I'm talking to you," she says, waving her hand in front of my face.My heart urged me to confess 'I missed you',my mind resisted but my eyes betrayed me and it revealed the depth of my longing for her.

"Wait,Are you okay?Why are you crying?"Vaishnavi questioned.

I reached out and took her hand saying "Can we walk for sometime?"She looked at me with a smile on her face and said "Sure Krish"

We walked through the streets holding each other's hands."Krish,I need to tell you something."Vaishnavi stated.I knew what she was gonna say.

"Subinay told me everything. It's okay, Vaishnavi,"I replied.

"Okay?You are not angry with me?"She stopped walking and asked.

"No,"I said.

"Where are we going?"She inquired.

"To our place,"I replied.She held my hand tight and said "Let's Go".We reached the playground and sat on our bench.Vaishnavi told me how she enjoyed there.Seeing her talking with me after a long time made me understand that joy often finds its meaning in the shadows of past sadness.

"I haven't been here since the day you left,"I confessed to her.

"Why?You said this place will make you feel better,"Vaishnavi asked me.

"Before our paths crossed,I chose this place to be alone but now, in your absence, it echoes with my loneliness,"I admitted.

She, who had been holding my hand until then, gently left it and said, "Krish, I may not be with you every time.

I'm really glad I can make you happy, but it's important for you to find happiness even when I'm not around."

"What do you mean?"

She came closer. "We're foolish to think only humans can make us happy," she said, her tone firm. "Remember the day we spent under the sky?"

"Yes,I do,"I replied.

"It made us happy too.There are things that can make us happy all over the world.We need to search for it."

I looked at her and said "But we cannot travel the whole world."Vaishnavi excitedly said "We don't need to travel the whole world,our town is enough."

She was about to do something, but I couldn't quite grasp what she was saying. "Krish, we still have holidays. How about we go and... say 'I love you'?"

"I love you?To whom?"I am confused.

She laughs "Look,tell me which made you happy when I was not around?"

"Sky. You told me that it has a healing effect and, actually, it worked," I replied.She pressed her palm on my cheek "Exactly Krish.If a person or anything else in our world becomes a source of courage for us, that is love."

Damn man.Whatever she says,touches my heart like a toddler's smile.I saw me in her eyes and held her hand on my cheeks "Don't dare to leave me ever."

She stood up "We will start today from the night sky.Are you ready for your first proposal to the sky?"

"Yes,Captain,"I laughed.The idea that she had shared was childish but all I thought was I could spend time with her.We decided to watch the night sky at her house that night.

We headed back from the playground "Vaishnavi,Do you follow every quote that you read?"I asked.

"Of course not," she replied."I don't adopt every quote, Krish. Our connection to quotes is shaped by our unique situations and personal connections."

I shook my head with confusion and said, "I didn't understand what you just said."

She laughs "I once saw a bunch of friends globetrotting, and it made me crave travel. A few days later, I stumbled upon a quote: 'By reading books, we can travel without moving an inch.' Inspired by that, I decided to follow the quote since I can't explore the world at the moment,"She replied.

"Uff, this is driving me crazy.That's right," I continued to stare at her and said, "My dad always talks like this with Chitra."

"I can say that Krish, he is a good person. There's something about him, a kind of quiet strength and unwavering kindness that makes him stand out,"Vaishnavi began, her words carrying a deep sense of respect.

"I don't know what he writes in that book, but I am curious to read it,"she continued."Have you ever asked him about it?" she inquired, leaning in closer.

"We need to stop talking about him",I retorted.

"But Krish..,"she began.

"We reached your home.Forget all that,I will join you at 7,"I said quietly,stopping her from talking.

"Okay Krish,"She said and went in. I got back home and let Chitra know about my plan to head to Vaishnavi's place at 7 p.m. Following that, I took a quick shower and switched into fresh clothes.

I don't know what he writes in that book, but I am curious to read it. Those words by her were running through my head.

"My dad's book was on the table, and I felt like flipping through it. As the wind rustled the pages, I noticed a word, 'Sravanth.' Intrigued, I was about to turn to that page.

Chitra entered the room and asked "Krish, are you leaving?".I fumbled "Yeah,Yeah, in a few minutes"

"What are you doing there?You never go to dad's table"She asked me,watching me near my dad's table.

"No,Nothing.I was just coming out of the room.Could you make some tea?".I came back without looking at it.

"Sure" she gazed in disbelief.

Chitra and I were having tea. "Krish,don't go near that book again."

"What does he write in that book?"I asked her.Chitra also never read it.

"Getting late,You need to go."Chitra said.I told her that I won't go there again to that place but all the way to Vaishnavi's home I was thinking about it.I erased all the thoughts and reached her home.

Mr.Deva received me "She is on the terrace Krish."

"Okay,thanks"I said and went on to the terrace.

"Krish,"he called me.

"Yes,Mr.Deva,"

"She always talks about you.You're her only friend," he said. "She hardly connects with anyone, not even with our family members. Thank you, Krish" He kissed me on the forehead.

"I'm glad to hear that, Mr.Deva," I replied with a broken voice. I wasn't sure why he got emotional.

"Okay,I will go to the terrace,"I said.

"Sure Krish,"He was looking at me with a very happy face when I was going.Vaishnavi was walking on the terrace "Hey Kiddo".She always welcomes me with that word.

"If you call me that again,I will leave"I teased."Sorry about that," she chuckled. "Can we watch the sky? It's full of stars now," she said, laying out the mat on the floor.We laid down on the floor and were staring at the sky. "Say something idiot,"she kicked me.

"Ouch! Let me watch the sky for sometime."I kicked her too.We both laughed by looking at the sky.

"You know, the day after I fought with my dad, I decided not to go to the playground anymore. I tried to find something else to distract myself," I confided.

She was already wet with tears when I started talking about cricket. "Krish,Please.."

"No No.Listen,that day I tried to do something and I realized that I know nothing."I replied.

"Then try to search."She got up and sat down.

"Search?"

"Krish, you started loving cricket and chose to learn it. There are so many things we love to do. We need to search for them. Why did you get stuck there? You can achieve something great, I believe in you."

I was looking at her with blurred vision. "We will talk about it later.Now close your eyes and think whether the night sky can make you happy or not" She diverted the topic.

As I embraced the darkness behind closed eyes, her memory accompanied me, and the night sky whispered promises of eternal joy.

I was still closing my eyes. "Krish, there are millions of people under this night sky. All of them are fighting for something in their own lives. But one day they win. When you win, be happy. When you lose, be patient. Yes, you lost that day, so be patient. Join the collective battles under this sky. Now, open your eyes, Krish,"she said.

Opening my eyes, the sky seemed to cradle me in its vastness. The beauty that unfolded before me painted the most beautiful canvas, and it seemed as if the sky had reserved its magnificence just for me.

With a happy voice I whispered "I love you,"to the sky.

"Say it aloud Krish",She stood up.She pulled me from the floor to stand.She shouted "Krish loves you sky." I loved her madness.

"I love you,"We both yelled loudly until our voices became hoarse.We went back to those lounger chairs.

Mr. and Mrs. Deva brought dinner to the terrace, the scent of their home-cooked meal mingling with the cool evening breeze. The sky above was adorned with a beautiful full moon.

"Mr. Deva, I really shouldn't stay," I murmured softly, feeling a pang of guilt tugging at my conscience. But he seemed oblivious to my reluctance, bustling about as he arranged plates and bowls with meticulous care, his movements a testament to his hospitality and warmth.

"Mr.Deva.."

"I hear you kid.I will tell your parents.Don't worry.Vaishu's mom cooks well."

Mrs. Deva flashed me a warm smile, her eyes twinkling with kindness as she gestured for me to take a seat. "Oh, nonsense, Krish. You must join us," she insisted, her voice carrying the gentle lilt of persuasion.

With a mat brought by Vaishnavi,we organized everything on its surface.We had dinner and Mr.Deva told about his childhood memories of how he got scolded by his parents.He consistently filled us with joy.

Vaishnavi said "My dad wrote a song, Krish".When she spoke those words, Mr&Mrs.Deva became silent, and their faces visibly dimmed.

"Not now Vaishu,He is getting late",Mr.Deva ignored to sing.

"No dad,he will stay,Please."Vaishnavi forced him.

"Okay,Okay."He started singing.

When the eyes were blur
I saw a different fear
The poet is telling me to wait
Reader is forcing me to get
The situation is a chaos,
But the power is in words.

"Alright, that's enough,"Mrs.Deva interrupted. "Vaishu, lend me a hand in clearing this up. Take them to the kitchen," she requested Vaishnavi.

I asked Mr.Deva "When did you write this song?"

He knelt down and said, "It's a song I wrote for Vaishu's mom. When Vaishnavi was in..."

"Stop it deva,"Mrs.Deva shouted.She was frightened by something.

"Let's head downstairs, Krish," he said.I told Vaishnavi and made my way back home.I was still processing why Vaishnavi's mom reacted like that.Mr.Deva was going to say something about Vaishnavi.

An hour later,Vaishnavi called me "Where will we go next?"I thought about asking her about what Uncle mentioned regarding her.I decided to ask her in person.

"I don't know.Can we just roam the town?"I asked.

"Okay.We will do it this weekend,"Vaishnavi replied.I hated the fact that I don't have answers for anything.I was pissed.I had waited to meet her on the weekend.I am not sure when I dozed off and I heard a voice in my head saying 'Krish.You need to go'.It reminded me a dream I had long time ago.

The funny part is, we always want to know things, even if it might hurt us.I thought the answer to that dream might lie in my dad's book or with Vaishnavi. But whatever it may be, I hope it won't hurt me.

It's Saturday Morning.Vaishnavi called me "Are you ready?"she asked me on the phone call,

"Yes,"I replied.

"Bring your cycle,We will start from my home."She asked.I was silent for a while "But you don't have a cycle."I replied.

"Don't you have? Kiddo".I told Chitra about this,and then I visited Vaishnavi's house.She was outside, waiting for me, and her mom waved at us from the doorstep and said "Don't be late, Vaishu"

She sat back on my cycle "All good,Go Krish."I started to move and She held my T Shirt from the back.In that moment, I realized that smiles can appear even when the heart is pounding and I wished for an endless road ahead.

"So where are we heading to?"I questioned her.Even she didn't know our endpoint, and she simply said, "Just go until you get tired"

We went so far away from our area.We spotted a place full of trees.I parked my cycle aside and decided to explore that area. Birds,wind and the light made us stay there for more time.

"Krish,take that stone,"Vaishnavi asked for the stone to write something on the tree. "Turn around Krish.See what I wrote later"

"Okay,I will,"I turned around.

"You can see now, Kiddo" She finished writing and it says "Vaishnavi and Krish loves you"

"Haha.That's true.I loved these trees,"I said.I took the stone and wrote those words on some other trees.Vaishnavi held my hand "Krish,This is also a place for you.Whenever you feel low,you can come here"

"Sure thing"

The places and things she shared with me undoubtedly brought about a sense of joy and the reason behind that joy was her presence beside me.

We are going back home on the cycle.Vaishnavi said "Krish,How lovely that tree grows in silence.If we are able to do that,we will grow as we grow up"

I didn't respond to her words. My dad spoke the exact same words to me when I was a kid. "Grow in silence,you will grow as you grow up."

"That place,I enjoyed it a lot"She rested her head on my back and fell asleep.

It started raining when we were halfway there.I stopped my cycle to park it aside until it stopped. "Krish,I will hold you tight.Go"Vaishnavi said.

"In the rain?"

"Yes.Go Krish",she excitedly insisted.

I grasped her hands and wrapped them securely around my waist, saying, "Hold on tight"She was shouting all the way "Ooh...".At that moment,I thought "This memory with her gives me love whenever I miss her or feel lonely and I silently confessed my love to sky 'I love you rain'"

"Vaishnavi,We have reached."I stopped my cycle.She got down from the cycle.

"Okay Krish, I'm sleepy. I'll call you later, okay?"She said sleepily.

"Sure, take care."

"Bye, Kiddo,"she said, heading inside.

In the rain,when she turned back to wave at me I saw the most beautiful girl ever.

I thought she would call me again before the weekend, but she never did. When I went to her house, they weren't there. I called her on my mom's phone, and Vaishnavi's mom answered, saying, "Hey, Krish"

"Hello Mrs. Deva, I visited your home but you were not there, so…" I replied, trailing off.

"We came to Vaishu's grandma's house,"She said.Vaishnavi never does that.She always tells me if she would go somewhere.

"Vaishnavi?"I asked her.

"She went out with her dad Krish. I'll let her know to call you," she informed me before ending the call.I haven't heard from Vaishnavi for so long.

After the holidays, she returned. Subinay and I resumed our routine of going to school from my house.

"Krish,Haven't you heard from Vaishnavi yet?"Subinay asked.

"No"

Vaishnavi was waiting for us at the playground in our school. She hadn't informed me about her return."Sorry Krish,I was busy," Vasihnavi said.Subinay was looking at us without saying a word.

"At least you need to say when you are returning"I said and left from there.We went back to our houses together, but not a single word was exchanged between us.

After the sunset,I went to the playground.Vaishnavi was already there and waiting for me.

"Why are you here?"I said without looking at her.She attempted to make a funny face to get my attention."This is our place,So I am here,"She replied.

I sat on the bench.She came closer "Sorry.Sorry.Sorry"

"You should have called me at the very least once.Don't do that again"I replied.

"Awww,Kiddo is so sweet," she laughs.

Vaishnavi's dad came to the ground and said loudly, "Vaishu, you need to go home right now."

"Mr.Deva,what happened?"

"Vaishu,Now.I told you to go," Uncle got angry.

"Dad, I am talking with him,"Vaishnavi said. I had never seen Uncle in that much tension before.She left by saying "I will talk with you tomorrow Krish"

"Mr.Deva,are you okay?Why are you yelling at her?"I questioned him.

"Sit Krish.You remembered the song that I sang that night?"He asked me.

"Yes,I do.You wrote it for Mrs.Deva,"I replied.

"Exactly son.I wrote it for her but it is about Vaishnavi.The toughest part we face in life is having to say something, even when we know it will hurt them,"he said.

He told the meaning of that song "The lyrics he wrote says–'When the eyes are filled with tears and fear.My heart tells me not to say it, but my brain insists. In those moments, my words either give her courage or cause pain'.That situation can only be managed with words.We are not happy Krish,just trying to be happy"

"What is that situation?"I asked him.He didn't answer that question.His phone rings,Vaishnavi's mom called him.

"No, I haven't spoken to him. I'm on my way home,"he replied.

"Mr.Deva,tell me.What is that situation?"I asked him aloud.

"I need to go, Krish"He stopped me from asking more questions. An hour later, I returned home,Chitra and

Mom packing our bags.

"Chitra,Are we going somewhere?"I questioned.She gave me the bag and said "Yes Krish,Pack your clothes in this"

"Where are we going?"

Uncle's(Mom's brother)health was not good,he is in hospital.We need to go and be there for them,Chitra replied.

"But the school just opened today" I ignored going with them.Dad just arrived home "We understand, but we have to go. We'll be back in 10 days. I've also spoken to your class teacher and Subinay"

"Chitra,I need to call Vaishnavi.Please",I requested her.She brought mom's mobile and I called Vaishnavi.Mr.Deva picked up.

"Tell me Krish,"he answered.

"Mr.Deva,Vaishnavi?"He called her and gave the phone.

"Vaishnavi,I am leaving town.I will return after 10 days."I told her.All she said was "Okay Krish,Take care" and ended the call.

That day,In the game of closing and opening my eyes, Every time I lost,my eyes reminded me of the words through the tears and it beat my heart saying "You don't know the answers for the words you heard again 'Sravanth' and 'We are not happy'."

4
Whispers of Remembrance

We reached my uncle's home.A sense of urgency propelled my parents to swiftly stow their luggage before dashing off to the hospital. Chitra and I stayed with my cousins and grandma.

Amidst laughter and whispered conversations, we sought solace in each other's company, our hearts heavy with concern for our uncle's well-being. As the evening unfolded, the air thickened with a blend of anticipation and apprehension, a delicate balance mirrored in the stories shared and the silent prayers offered up for his recovery.

"Krish, are you studying well?" Grandma asked, her eyes peering over her glasses.Chitra came in the middle "He was but not now".Grandma's expression shifted, her brows furrowing with concern. She turned her gaze to Chitra, silently urging her to explain further.

"He is studying well but not as good as before,"Chitra said to her.Grandma gestured for me to sit beside her,her expression a blend of gentle inquiry and genuine care. Unsure of what to say, I settled in beside her, readying myself for the conversation ahead.

"You don't need to explain anything Krish.Go and take some rest"Grandma said.I didn't slept well for 5 days in my uncle's house.The streets I walked to,the trees I passed to,The sky I loved,The people I liked never gave me any answers for the questions I had.

One morning, I awoke to find my grandmother standing before me. Still groggy from sleep, I asked, "Grandma, what's going on?"

Grandma and I were walking in the garden and she said "I've been noticing that since the day you all arrived,you haven't exchanged a single word with your dad."

"Grandma,Please.I can't talk about it right now,"I tried to stop her from talking about dad.

She replied"You don't need to say anything.Just listen to my words.I don't know how your dad behaved with you but you need to know this,He knows what he is doing."

She became highly emotional, and as she spoke about my dad, her eyes mirrored the same intensity as when she narrated the story of Ramayana to Chitra and me.The respect and love.I left from there and she called me "Krish, I am always sad why your father was not born in my womb but he is my son-in-law and he calls me 'mom'"

"Why are you saying this to me,Grandma?"

"One day,you will be so glad that he is your father,"she replied and went to her room.When we are hating a person,we just don't listen and we don't try to understand the good things about them.All we remember is the hatred and what makes us to hate them.

Uncle was discharged and he needed bed rest.Mom told grandma that uncle was completely fine.

Chitra was packing the luggage in the room "Krish,pack your bag too,we will leave tomorrow."

"Already?"

"Yes Krish.Uncle is fine,"Chitra said.I sat in front of my bag, pondering over Vaishnavi, feeling utterly perplexed by her father's words.The power was gone,no lights.In the dark silence,her memories and questions filled my sight

'We are not happy.'

"Krish,What are you doing in the dark?Come outside.It's raining,"Grandma called me.Everyone were enjoying the rain from the balcony.The rain poured heavily, bringing dust inside through the windows. We rushed in and closed the doors.

Dad remarked on the heavy rain, hoping for better weather tomorrow.Mom inquired about our departure time, to which Dad responded, '7 PM.'

The following day, dark clouds still hung in the sky.I was afraid that we wouldn't go that night.I sat outside on the stairs and I was watching those dark clouds and Chitra from behind said "Don't worry, we are leaving today."

"Really?Dad said that?"

"Yeah,he just booked the tickets for 12PM",Chitra replied.We are about to leave in the afternoon.

She sat beside "He changed his mind.I think because of the weather.It's better to leave in the daytime."Chitra and I talked for a while and we packed everything to leave at 12PM.

While we were in the room, Grandma visited us. I thought she would scold me, but she just said, "Krish, remember my words, okay?" and told Chitra to take care of me.

"Chitra,It's time" mom shouted.

"Coming mom,Krish help me with the luggage",Chitra asked for help.Grandma was looking at me and smiling.I pondered asking her about the name I had come across in my dad's book.

"Krish,take those bags.What are you thinking?"Chitra called me.Dad sought blessings from Grandma, and Chitra and I headed to Uncle 's room. "Take care of your health, Uncle," We said.We started at 11:40PM and the bus was on time.The window seat always makes me lost in thoughts.I fell asleep as soon as our journey started.

Rubbing the sleep from my eyes, I blinked blearily and glanced around, trying to make sense of my surroundings. The bus had come to an unexpected halt, the engine's hum silenced, replaced by an eerie stillness.

My gaze followed Chitra's pointing finger, and my heart sank as I saw the obstacle blocking our path—a massive tree, sprawled across the road like a fallen giant, its branches reaching out as if in protest against our passage. It was a scene of unexpected obstruction, a natural barricade halting our journey in its tracks.

The driver, faced with this unforeseen obstacle, made the decision to divert onto an alternate route, steering the bus away from the fallen tree and onto a different path.We reached home at 11PM.

"Krish and Chitra,go and sleep,"Mom said.If I'm not feeling tired, Chitra mentioned that I can attend school tomorrow.I waited for the next day to meet Vaishnavi and I didn't sleep the whole night.Early in the morning I called Subinay and asked him to go to school together.Later,I called Vaishnavi but she didn't answered.

Subinay and I went to school early.We were going on cycle and I asked "Subinay,I haven't talked with Vaishnavi.She is not responding to the calls"

"She went to her relatives's wedding Krish and asked me to pass this information when you are here,"Subinay replied.

"What?"I stopped my cycle.

"Yes Krish,she will return in two days.Why you stopped,it's getting late," Subinay hits my cycle with his.

We got to school, and I wasn't interested in classes. During lunch,Subinay and I were chatting.

"Subinay,I am worried about my life,"I murmerred.If the ones we care about and like aren't around, especially when we are sad, the journey of our thoughts is always trying for a destination where we hate us.

"The answer for your question was shown by Vaishnavi.You changed a lot after you met her but you are still missing something.Aren't you?"Subinay asked me back.

"Yes"

"You will get the answer for that question when you talk to your parents Krish" He told me that and left me alone.The day was about to get over and I was waiting for her.I went to bed happy, knowing that I just had to wait one more day to meet her.

"Krish,Subinay is waiting outside,Go" Chitra shouted from the hall room while I was changing..He came early wantedly to get me scolded.As always we went together to school and we were missing Vaishnavi.In the first period, the math class was in session, and the teacher was about to take attendance.

The school monitor came to the class and excused the teacher "Krish,Your dad is here.In the principal's office"

I asked the teacher to allow me and she noted my attendance.En route to the office, I inquired with the monitor about the reason for my dad's presence.He said that he doesn't know either.

I went inside the office.

"Krish,you need to go with your dad,"the Principal said.I was about to ask why but dad held my hand and said "Thank you mam"

He dragged me outside and I yelled at him to leave me.He stood silently.

"I don't want to come with you"I said.He didn't move a bit.I looked at him,into his eyes.My dad's eyes filled with tears, resisting their path down his cheeks.

"Krish,you need to go" someone shouted from behind.It's Subinay, he came running from the classroom.

"What happened,Subinay?"

"Krish,when you left they took attendance.The teacher told the class..,"Subinay was crying.

I dashed forward, my heart pounding with each step. The haunting words echoed in my mind, "Krish, you need to go" This time, it wasn't just a dream. Tears welled up, blurring my vision, as Subinay's words resurfaced: "The teacher said Vaishnavi had died."

Dad scooped me up on his bike as I ran.Arriving at Vaishnavi's house, I found her dad packing everything up.

"Krish,we are sorry,"Holding my fist hard wiping my tears.He said "Krish,we are sorry"

"Why are you sorry, Mr. Deva?" I demanded, my voice trembling with both fear and anger. "Krish, please," he said, his eyes pleading with me to understand something I couldn't yet grasp.

"Fuck, tell me it is a lie," I raised my voice, the desperation in my tone echoing through the room. Vaishnavi's mom was sitting on the couch, her face pale and drained of all color. I couldn't believe what I was hearing, and I needed someone to tell me it wasn't true.

I knelt at her feet, my hands gripping the edge of the couch so tightly "Mrs. Deva, tell me it's a lie. Where is she?" I searched her eyes for any hint of hope.

She looked down at me, her eyes welling up with tears. She reached out and gently wiped away the tears streaming down my face. Her touch was soft and comforting, but it did nothing to quell the storm raging inside me.

"Stop that and tell me, where is she?" I shouted, my voice cracking under the weight of my anguish. I hit the couch with my fist, the sound sharp and startling in the heavy silence of the room. "Where is Vaishnavi?" My voice broke on her name.

Mr. Deva looked away, unable to meet my eyes. The silence that followed was deafening, filled with the unspoken truth that none of us wanted to face. Mrs. Deva's shoulders shook with silent sobs.

"Krish, it's okay." She hugged me tightly. I screamed, a raw, guttural sound,filled with all the pain that I couldn't put into words. She held me even tighter, her embrace a desperate attempt to contain my breaking heart. "It's okay, it's okay, Krish," she repeated, her voice a soothing whisper in my ear, though her own tears flowed freely.

"She succumbed to brain cancer," Mrs. Deva said, her voice heavy with sorrow. The words hung in the air like a weight, crushing me with their finality. I felt as if the ground had been pulled out from beneath me, leaving me adrift in a sea of grief.

"We knew we would lose her, Krish," she continued, her eyes filled with tears. "But that doesn't make it any easier."

"You were the only person she liked to talk to," Mrs. Deva said, her voice trembling with emotion. "We are so grateful that you were able to spend time with her, to bring her some joy in her final days."

"Every day she used to say, 'Dad, I don't have hope that I will survive,'" he said, his words heavy with the weight of a father's heartbreak. "But one day, she said, 'Dad, I want to spend time and live with Krish.'"

Tears pricked at the corners of my eyes as I realized the depth of Vaishnavi's love for me, a love so fierce and unyielding that it had carried her through even the darkest days of her illness. She had faced the prospect of death with courage and dignity, her only wish to be by my side, to share whatever time we had left together.

The voice of her,the memories of her and the words of her were hitting my heart. "Mr.Deva, When was she..?"

"Two days ago,we buried her in our hometown Krish,"Mr.Deva replied.I was angry with him, but I understood why he didn't let me know.

"We are moving Krish.Today" Mrs.Deva said.

"Please, don't go. Why?" I pleaded, the words catching in my throat as a wave of panic washed over me. I couldn't bear the thought of losing them too, of being left alone in a world that suddenly seemed so empty.

"Don't go," I whispered, the words barely more than a broken plea. "I'll be alone again."

Mrs. Deva knelt down beside me, wrapping her arms around me in a tight embrace. "I'm so sorry, Krish," she said softly, her voice filled with sorrow. "But we have to go. It's what's best for us."

"We'll always be here for you, Krish," she said, her voice choking with emotion. "No matter where we go, you'll always have a family in us."

"You can call us anytime,son.If you need us, just give us a call.We will come for you."Mr.Deva said.I hugged them both "I am afraid,I don't want to be lonely Mr.Deva."

He patted me gently on the back. "You will be alright, Krish," he assured me. I stayed with them until evening, watching as they started to pack up and prepare to leave. Dad, Mom, Chitra, and Subinay were all there.

Mrs.Deva reached into her bag and pulled out a small mobile phone, holding it out to me with trembling hands. "Vaishnavi asked me to give you this, Krish," she said.

On that day, I understood how everything can change in a single day. The people who helped me smile were no longer with me.

I often think about how it would feel to lose someone I loved, and that day, I found the answer. It's a feeling of emptiness. My mind came to a standstill, and my body simply told me, "You have to accept what just happened."

The thought of waking up tomorrow with a feeling of not having that person beside me,frightened me.Losing her reminded me that I lost myself.

Vaishnavi asked me to give you this,Krish.

It's 1AM and I took the phone that Mrs.Deva gave me.Dad was still awake and writing his book in the hall room.I unlocked the phone and it's completely empty.

I will write everything in it

I opened the notepad on that phone.There's a note that says "Open the audio"

I opened the audio and plugged the earphones.It has only one file.

I clicked on the audio file, my fingers shaking as I hovered over the play button. With a deep breath, I pressed it, and the sound of Vaishnavi's voice filled the room.**"Hey Kiddo."**

I resumed.

Hey kiddo,If you're hearing this, it means I won't be there for you.Krish,you are the best thing that happened to me.

I am not old enough but I need to tell you this.We just spent half of our parents' age.How can we decide that we can't have happiness anymore? You failed in achieving your passion but you still have your life in your hands.It's the heart Krish,we can find happiness anywhere.

Sobbing "Don't cry",Mrs.Deva from behind.

I always wished that I would see you success in your life and what you are going to be but I am..

Krish,you are the best character that I haven't read in any book.Promise me that you should always be smiling.You always ask me why I love words.Words are shadows of humans Krish.It's stays with us forever.Krish,Now I am saying the words to you that stays with you even when I am not with you,I love you.I love you krish.

I know that I am gonna die and I am not mad about it until I met you.Coming back to my home everyday after school,I wish that I want to live.You are the person I would have in my eyes before I close it forever.I am really hating that I can't hear your voice anymore.Whenever you are in the playground,around

trees and every time you see the sky remember I am right there beside you.

When I asked you what life is,you answered,life is maybe moments.If life is a series of moments,then there is no true end.I always live in your moments.

Thank you Krish.For meeting me,scolding me,laughing with me,holding me and crying for me.

Mom I can't...

The audio ended and I began to cry aloud, awakening everyone. Chitra rushed to my side and pulled me close. "Krish, it's okay."

"Chitra, I'm lost. I don't know what to do. I feel like I'm slowly falling apart inside," I lamented.She stayed with me the entire night,I slept on her lap.The only word that everyone says when we are feeling low is 'it's okay'.That word really holds the heaviness.Mom woke me up in the morning and my body was really burning.They took me to the hospital and they really worried.

I was in the hospital the entire morning.The doctor came to me "Hello Krish,How are you feeling now?"

"Good,thank you."

"Krish,when was the last time you got a fever?"Doctor asked me.I replied that I had a year ago.

As he measured the temperature, he said, "It's really annoying , isn't it? We need to stay at home until it's cured."

"Yes,It is."

"So,you visited the same clinic that time?"He questioned.He sat on the chair in front of me.

"No.I never saw you before" I replied, as I don't know him."Then answer me Krish,Who Am I?What's my job?"He continued questioning.

"You are a doctor,you cure people."

"Exactly Krish. Days can make you weak, but you'll encounter different people who can help cure that. Again,you need to live your life on your own. You just need to say one thing to those people, just words," and the doctor and I simultaneously uttered those words: "Thank you".

He noticed my teary eyes and said the familiar words, 'It's okay.' Since the day I met Vaishnavi, words have consistently been chasing me. Initially, I believed they were just stirring questions within me, but in reality, they have been a source of healing.

'Words are shadows of humans Krish'

I went to the playground,to our place.I asked the sky "She said that you can make me happy,Right? Tell me,What should I do now?I need her.Now I can only see her when I close my eyes".Everyone told me to mingle with people so I can never feel sad but Vaishnavi asked me why only people.

The next few days of my school felt like an empty jungle.One day Subinay fired on me in the class "How much longer?" at the top of his lungs.

"Stop,"I said without looking at him.

"Stop? Vaishnavi was my friend too.I know how much she means to you but you need to accept and move on".He pushed me "I am talking with you."

I grabbed his collar "I'm trying, but I can't."

He embraced me tightly and my tears cascaded on his shoulders.Subinay wiped my tears "Vaishnavi hates when you cry.She helped you when you were facing hard times.Now you are in hard times again.Show me what she taught you."

Every time I make my way from the ground to the house, the path throws questions at me. However, this time, I had the answer.Thinking about someone we've lost weighs on our hearts, but the memory of their words brings tears to our eyes.

Her words are the things that make me cry but if I think about them, they are also the things that make me heal.Like she said,words stay with us forever.

I went home to listen to her words again.Her voice brought back memories of the day when she posed questions to me.One day she asked..

"Why are you always thinking,Kiddo?"Vaishnavi asked.

"I know what happened,happened, but don't know how to move on,"I replied.

"Okay lemme tell you this.Does the pain go away if we cry?or will memories die?Can new memories make the pain go away?or Do you have to erase the old memories in your heart to make new memories?Can't new sweet memories wipe away the tears of bitter memories?" She questioned me.

I fell asleep thinking that day along with the earphones in my ear.That day, it struck me - the night isn't for sleeping or giving rest to our body; it's for a self-cuddle.

When I met her,my mask unfolds,now she is my broken mask and I decided to live with her words.

5

Pages of Healing

It's been months since she left us.Hearing her voice every day is a habit I've fine-tuned. Accepting what happened, though, is not something that happens quickly. Instead of going to the playground, I used to go to the places that Vaishnavi and I loved.

After school,I take my cycle and go there.I sit near the trees and talk to them.Talking to Trees like that causes me a globus sensation.

School announced the pre-finals examinations for my 10th standard.On that day, I asked the trees "If she is here, we may hit the books together.When I talk to you, it feels like I'm talking to her.You guys both listen to me.You remember? How does she call me 'hey kiddo'? I am trying to move on but I don't know,see, I am crying."

I felt a profound sadness realizing how many people beneath this sky are enduring pain.In the midst of many people around me, all I grasp is the shared reality of their suffering.Many questions were prompted by that thought.

I can spend the entire day with the sky, trees, and sometimes rain, but the moment I go to sleep feels like hell.Whenever I try to convince myself to forget about her, her memory comes rushing back to me.

Those thoughts are my tears, those tears block my eyes and don't let me sleep. If I think about it, breathing and crying will sustain our lives.It is true that tears of pain are painful, but not weakness.

My grandma once said, "If we cry, we forget the pain." But I didn't want to forget Vaishnavi. The thought of her lingered in my mind, even as I walked back home.

When I arrived, Dad was waiting for me. I headed straight to my bedroom, seeking solace in its familiarity. Chitra soon came to my door and softly said, "Dad is calling you."

I shook my head, unable to face him just yet.

"Krish, please. Just come and stay there for a moment," she pleaded.

Reluctantly, I walked to the living room where Dad had muted the TV. His gaze was fixed on me with a mix of concern and expectation.

"I heard that your pre-finals are starting soon," Dad said, his voice carrying a tone of both inquiry and command.

"Yes, Dad," Chitra answered, her voice trembling slightly.

"Krish? Can't you hear me?" Dad's voice raised, his patience wearing thin. "I'm talking to both of you."

Chitra stepped back.

"Don't talk like that with him, we know what happened right?", Mom said. He told Chitra to make me study.They didn't let me talk with him,they knew I would fight.

"What's his problem Chitra?"I asked.

"Nothing,go to your room,"Chitra pushed me out of his way.Mom stopped him from talking "You know he is not talking to you, why are you shouting , you didn't even start the conversation yet?"

I ignored him and rushed myself to the bedroom and he said

"It's been months since that girl died. Look at him,wandering around, staying on the terrace, always plugged into those earphones."

Mom's soothing tone tried to bridge the chasm between us. "Calm down. He'll be okay."

But Dad's frustration boiled over. "How many times does he need to listen to that voice note?" With a furious snatch, he ripped the mobile and earphones from my hands, his anger palpable.

"What are you doing?" I shouted, my voice cracking under the weight of my own despair.

"No more mobile," Dad roared. "Focus on your exams. No more cycling; I'll drop you. After school, stay home and study." He tossed my mobile into his locked drawer, as though the metal could contain my anguish.

"Are you mad? Why do you always try to hurt me? I hate this! I don't want to hate you. You're the reason I'm like this now. Why can't you just kill me instead?" My voice rose to a wail, raw and desperate.

Mom's hand struck my face with a sharp crack, and the sting was a harsh reminder of how lost I felt. "Krish, stop!"

"You think this slap can hurt me?" I exploded, my voice tearing through the room like a storm, raw and furious. The sting on my cheek was nothing compared to the ache that had hollowed out my chest for months. My rage came pouring out, unchecked, a torrent that had been dammed up for far too long. "I've endured more than that, and you know it! You took away cricket, the one thing that kept me sane, the one thing that made me feel alive. And now you think this is how you fix things? By shutting me down even more?"

The words clawed their way out of me, louder, fiercer, like a roar that had been buried in my throat, growing louder with every breath. My voice cracked, then built again, a crescendo of all the anger, all the pain. "Vaishnavi... she was more than just a friend. She was my hope! My guide through this mess you've created! She taught me what love is, what it means to feel alive! And you... what do you say to all of that?"

I could hear my own breath, ragged and heavy, feel my chest heaving with each word that left my lips. "You stand there, and all you have to say is 'It's been months'? That's it? 'It's been months'?" I was shouting now, my voice cracking into a thousand jagged pieces. "You think time can erase what she meant to me? What she gave me?"

The room seemed to shrink with every word, the walls pushing in, tightening around us. I felt my throat burn, my words cutting through the air like shards of glass. "She loved me!" I yelled, my voice breaking, splintering into the heavy silence that followed. It wasn't just a statement; it was an accusation, a plea, a confession. "Do you hear me? She loved me!"

My voice echoed off the walls, vibrating through the floors and the bones of this house that had never felt like home. And in that moment, I felt my words reach them... Mom, Dad, Chitra... the full weight of my grief crashing over them like a tidal wave. Their faces were etched with shock, eyes wide and wet, caught in the crossfire of my pain.

The room fell into an unbearable silence, heavy and thick, like the air before a storm. Dad stood there, his face drained of color, eyes wide but unable to meet mine. His mouth opened slightly, as if searching for words that just wouldn't come—only a heavy breath that carried all the weight of his regret and unspoken sorrow. He wasn't the same towering figure who barked orders and slammed doors; he was just a father lost in the wreckage of his own mistakes, realizing too late the depth of the chasm he'd created.

Mom's hands, still trembling from the slap, slowly lowered to her side. She wasn't looking at Dad anymore; her eyes were locked on me, filled with a mixture of shock, hurt, and something deeper—a kind of guilt that seemed to stretch back through time, over all the moments she hadn't understood or hadn't been able to fix. She'd always been the bridge between us, the gentle voice trying to stitch together what had been torn apart, but now she was quiet too. Her lips parted as if to say something, anything, to reach out across the widening distance between us, but no words came. She was searching my face for answers in the pain that poured from my eyes, but there were none to be found.

Chitra hovered nearby, her lips pressed tightly together as if to keep from crying herself. She took a step toward me, her eyes brimming with concern and confusion, but then hesitated. She wanted to bridge the gap, to be the comfort that neither Mom nor Dad could offer right now, but she knew that this moment wasn't for her to fix. She felt it in the room—the kind of quiet that comes not from peace but from the eye of a storm. The tension hummed like a live wire, snapping and crackling in the spaces between us.

The walls seemed to shrink around us, pulling in closer with the weight of the unsaid, the unreleased. The curtains, usually fluttering with life, hung motionless, heavy with the weight of what had just been spoken. Even the clock on the wall ticked cautiously, as if aware that each second was deepening the divide. Each tick was a reminder of how time was moving forward, dragging us with it, even as we stood frozen in this moment of shared anguish.

And in that agonizing silence, it felt like the entire house was holding its breath, bracing itself, afraid that even the slightest sound would shatter whatever fragile thread still held us together. The world outside seemed muted and far away, almost unreal, like the distant murmur of another life where children playing in the distance, a bird chirping, the faint hum of a motorbike passing by—all oblivious to the implosion happening within these four walls.

My tears, hot and relentless, fell freely now, like rain hitting dry earth after a long, desolate drought. The wet streaks on my cheeks burned, each one a reminder of the depth of the loss I was drowning in. They watched, unable to turn away, as if my tears were a revelation, exposing everything we'd been too afraid to confront. For them, my tears were something new, a rare glimpse into the churning depths I'd kept hidden for too long. And they all stood there, looking for a sign, a word, or a breath to break this unbearable stillness.

Dad's shoulders slumped, his hands hung limply at his sides like he didn't know what to do with them. The anger that had flared so violently just moments ago seemed to have drained away, leaving behind only the hollow shell of a man who had tried and failed to understand his own son. His lips trembled as if he wanted to speak, but he stayed silent, as if sensing that anything he might say would only deepen the wound.

Mom, too, seemed lost in her own thoughts, her fingers twitching slightly like she wanted to reach out, but something held her back,perhaps the realization that this wasn't something that could be touched or healed with a mother's comforting hand. She stood there, helpless, watching her son unravel, feeling every piece of his breaking heart as if it were her own.

And then there was Chitra, her face twisted in a strange mix of empathy and helplessness. She wanted to be the one to make everything okay again, to be the glue that would hold us all together. She stepped forward once more, her voice soft and trembling, "Krish, wait..." But I shook my head, cutting her off.

"Leave me, Chitra. I need to be alone. I'll go to Subinay's house," I said, my voice breaking as I wiped away the relentless stream of tears. I turned and walked away, feeling the weight of their stares on my back, knowing they were searching for something—anything—to say, but there was nothing left in the room except the echo of my words and the heavy, unyielding silence that followed.

And as I stepped out, the house stood behind me, not as a home anymore but as a witness to a pain so deep, it had silenced even the walls. A place where, for a brief moment, time had stood still, holding its breath for the tears of a son and the unspoken regrets of a family.

He was already at his house's doorstep. "Your mom just called,Krish,"I requested him to go for a walk together.We went to the playground and sat there.

"Krish?"He called me.

"We will talk about it later,not now,"I asked him to be silent.He didn't talk about anything for an hour.

"Krish,it's getting late,"he said.

"Subinay,lemme ask you this.I never saw you crying for Vyshnavi or feeling sad.You are also close to her,"I asked him.

He smiled at me and said "If I cry with you too, who will take care of you?".That day I realized that we cry not only with our eyes but also with our hearts like him.Subinay wiped my tears and hugged me.His phone started ringing.

"Krish,Your mom is calling,"he asked me to talk.I ignored.He answered the call.The eyes that said it won't cry in front of me till then,filled with an ocean of tears.

"What happened?"I questioned him.

"You need to go,Your father collapsed with a heart attack.Run Krish".He held my hand and ran with me.When we reached, there was an ambulance.

"What are you looking at?Get in the ambulance,"Mom pulled me to her side with shedding tears.In the ambulance,my dad was laid down next to me.I don't understand what they are doing.I was afraid to see my dad like that.All the way to hospital,the sound of mother's cry, the fear in sister's eyes.Not a drop of tear came from my eyes but I don't know what my heart doing,a blur video was playing around me.

Mom called Uncle and Grandma.Doctors took dad to the operation theater.Doctor asked "How did it happen?Trouble at home?".Mom looked at me without saying anything and said "No doctor, nothing like that".

After a while, the nurse said "Don't worry mam, He is completely fine.He will be discharged after a couple of days."

Uncle visited the hospital that night, his face etched with concern. "Is he okay now?" he asked, his voice trembling with worry.

Mom looked up from her seat, her eyes reflecting exhaustion and relief. "Yes, they said he needs to be under observation for a few days."

Chitra, her eyes wide and anxious, ran to Uncle. "Uncle, he collapsed while writing his book," she said, her voice catching with emotion.

I moved closer to Chitra, sensing something was off. She looked at me, puzzled. "What did you just say?" I asked, a knot of fear tightening in my stomach.

Mom intervened quickly. "Mom, please stop. Chitra, could you please tell me?" I asked, trying to keep my voice steady.

Chitra hesitated, her eyes darting between me and Mom. After a moment, she spoke, her voice barely above a whisper. "Yes, Krish. After you left home, he went to his room and started writing. A few minutes later, he suddenly screamed in pain and collapsed."

I called Subinay "Subinay,I am at the hospital, can you come and drop me at home?"

Mom snapped, declaring firmly, "You're not going anywhere." Sensing the tension, Chitra stepped in, urging, "Mom, please calm down." Ignoring her plea, I swiftly snatched the keys from Chitra's hand and hurriedly left.

Subinay arrived at the hospital and phoned me from outside. As we made our way home, he turned to me and asked, "How's uncle holding up?"

"He is fine.Watch the road,"I replied.

"Why are you going home now?" He asked me, but I remained silent. I politely asked him to give me some space. He dropped me off and waited for me at his house.

I entered the room, accidentally knocking over the chair and pens. On the table, the book lay open, its pages fluttering in the air.I opened the first page, I saw the same name again "Sravanth".

I took a seat on the chair opposite the table, where my dad used to sit and started reading.

Feeling lost and betrayed by Sravanth's actions, I find myself in a tough spot. His business troubles drained my savings, leaving me financially strained. Despite reaching out, he hasn't responded to my calls or messages for days. This has led to frequent fights at home, with tensions running high.

In an attempt to start afresh, I suggested to Jayanthi that we move to a new town. However, she's reluctant to leave. This adds to the stress and uncertainty about our future.

My main concern is my children's well-being. Despite the turmoil, I still consider Sravanth a friend, but his betrayal hurts. It's daunting to think about breaking the news to Krish, but I know it's necessary for his sake.

No matter where we end up, my priority is ensuring my children have what they need for a stable and secure future.

-Vyas

I never thought I'd find myself in this situation again. Today, my worst fear came true when Krish asked me to buy him a Cricket Kit. It's something I can't afford, and I don't know how to break it to him.

The moment I looked into his hopeful eyes and said I couldn't buy it for him, I felt like a failure as a parent. I remembered my own childhood, watching my father struggle to provide for me, and I promised myself that my children would never go without.

But now, because of Sravanth's actions, I can't give Krish the happiness he deserves. I feel like I'm letting him down, and the weight of that responsibility is crushing.

Blaming Sravanth for all of this only adds to my frustration and anger. It's like I'm trapped in a never-ending cycle of disappointment and regret, and I don't

know how to break free from it.I am living in hell.

-Vyas

Everyday I can't see him silent like that and not talking to me.The only time I see him with my eyes is when he is sleeping.When he was arguing with me,tears would come to my eyes but the thought of my son growing up gives me joy.

Krish often visits the playground, a place where I hoped we could connect and spend time together. But today, when I mustered the courage to join him and sit close, I found him chatting happily with a girl from his class.

The longing to talk to my son, to bridge the gap that has grown between us, is overwhelming. It's a painful reminder of how much we've drifted apart, and how much I yearn to reclaim the closeness we once shared.

-Vyas

Upon my return home, I found Jayanthi in tears. When I inquired about the reason, she revealed that she had a fight with Krish earlier, and he left, expressing that we don't care about him.I can't tell him why,I can't make him understand without giving a reason.

As he cried in front of me, pouring out his emotions, it felt like my heart was shattering into pieces.Does he understand his father?

-Vyas

My love,Jayanthi, is asking and fighting about my writings.How can I explain to her that these are the words that I find challenging to express directly to our son.

I know he doesn't want to talk to me, so I yell at him every time he comes so late.At Least then he talks to me when we have a fight.

Looking at my beautiful son every day and writing this book makes my eyes teared up. I can't remember anything but regret that I am hurting him.

I always hold my tears and try to not cry.Time flies faster when we cry.I don't want it.It is enough to watch my son like this all night.I know he will understand me one day for sure.

-Vyas

Watching Subinay and Vaishnavi spending time with Krish, studying and hanging out together, fills me with conflicting emotions. On one hand, I'm grateful that he has friends who care about him and keep him company. But on the other hand, it stirs up a longing in me—a desire to turn back time and become a child again, just so I can be by Krish's side as a friend.

Every time I see them together, a silly thought crosses my mind: I wish I could be a child again, so I could join in their games and laughter. I imagine myself wiping Krish's tears when he's feeling down, sharing secrets, and feeling the warmth of his cheeks as we laugh and play together.

It's a whimsical notion, I know. But in those moments, I yearn for the simplicity of childhood, when friendship was uncomplicated and love knew no bounds. And more than anything, I long to be the friend that Krish needs, offering comfort, support, and unwavering companionship in his journey through life.

-Vyas

Today Sravanth's business partners enquired about him.They asked me to pay the money and I was paying them every month.

Krish watched us in that situation.What else can I do?What will Krish think if he knows that I am repaying the debt of Sravant?How can I say that I am doing this for Sravanth?What if he asks me, "Why are you thinking this way about a friend who cheated on you?"

-Vyas

Mr.Deva called me today and told me about Vaishnavi.My hands shivered and I couldn't even utter a word to him when he said about his daughter's condition.

The question of how to tell my son about his friend's death convulsed me.When I saw him coming inside the principal's office, I prayed this cannot be real.I recognized his friends' ability to make him happy which I cannot do.

But now,one of them is gone, he can't stand it.A few years back, I worried he wouldn't change, but now it's hard to picture him being like that again.

I couldn't bear the thought that my friend had cheated on me and left me but my son lost his friend forever.How will he bear this pain?

I want to hug him and say I'm here.

-Vyas

I got a call from the school that the pre-finals will start soon.I was scared,he couldn't concentrate on his studies.He is not in a situation to listen to me if I talk to him softly.

I had no choice but to talk to him with anger.The tears in his eyes tells me that he is hurting more than before.

Then it dawned on me, when we're unable to pursue activities that bring us joy, the pain can be overwhelming. Yet, amidst this ache, we often find solace in new connections, individuals who inadvertently alleviate the discomfort we feel.

Vaishnavi helped him to alleviate his pain but now she was the pain to him.

God,why are you making my son suffer like this?

Whenever I lay eyes on him, it reminds me that I am not a good dad to him.

-Vyas

Those are the last words he wrote before he collapsed.My happiness started dropping as tears.I closed that book with a smile on my face.I called Subinay "Can we go and see my dad?"

"Sure,let's go," he said with a doubtful face.

When we reached the hospital, I dashed to see him, brimming with happiness.

The happiness that I don't have a reason to hate him anymore.The happiness that I know how much he loves me.The happiness that he has always been a good father to me and always will be.

My tears glistened in my eyes, mirroring the bright smile adorned the face.

"Mom, Can I go and talk to him?"I asked.

"With Whom?"mom questioned.

"I want to talk to dad mom,"I replied.She was confused and said "Sure,of course."

Entering the room, I found him unconscious. I took a seat beside him and gently held his hand. I remembered all the words I had spoken to him, as I am holding his hand.

As memories flooded back, tears spilled onto his hand, my sobs muffled against his comforting palm.

"Krish?" Dad woke up, his voice weak but filled with concern.

I quickly wiped my tears and looked at him, forcing a smile. "Are you okay, Krish?" he asked, his grip tightening around my hand.

"I am sorry, Dad." As soon as I said that word, I understood it's true weight,meaning and how beautiful the word sorry is.

He squinted, trying to focus on my face. "I can't see you properly, Krish," he said.

With tissues in hand, I delicately dabbed away his tears. "Now you can see me, Dad," I said, smiling at him.

Immediately after wiping his eyes, happiness burst from them, and he said, "Smile once again."

"Dad?"

"Smile once, Krish. It's been years since I saw you smile," he replied.

I smiled, a genuine smile that reached my eyes.

"You know what makes a heart melt?" he questioned softly.

"What?" I asked, leaning in closer.

"The smile of others, especially the smiles of their children," he replied, his eyes twinkling with emotion.

"I just witnessed it, Dad," I said, feeling a warmth spread through my chest. "Take it easy, Dad. The doctor mentioned we'll be heading home soon," I said, offering a gentle reminder for him to relax.

He didn't let go of my hand. "I will, but stay here for some time," he pleaded softly.

"I'm not going anywhere, Dad," I assured him, settling back into the chair.

We sat in comfortable silence, the bond between us growing stronger with each passing moment. I was there with him until he fell asleep, his breathing becoming steady and calm. As I watched him sleep, I felt a profound sense of peace. We had faced so much, but in that moment, I knew we would be okay. Our love and forgiveness had mended the deepest wounds, and we had found our way back to each other.

6
Under the Canopy of Memories

❦

When my father returned home after being discharged, I found myself lost in a heavy silence. Words seemed to curl up and die in my throat. I couldn't even look him in the eye, let alone talk to him. For days, I drifted through the house, skirting around him like a ghost in my own home, feeling his presence but never meeting it. I'd glance his way, catch his tired eyes looking back, and quickly turn away. I didn't know what to say, how to fill the void between us. It felt like my voice had left me, taking with it all the things I needed to say.

But somehow, after what felt like forever, I found myself talking to him again—small words, cautious words. I didn't know why, maybe out of habit or perhaps because the silence was becoming too loud. Still, it wasn't easy. Each conversation felt like I was tiptoeing on broken glass, afraid that any wrong step would shatter whatever fragile peace we had left.

One morning, I woke up early, my body moving on autopilot, heading for the door to fetch the newspaper. As I reached out, Dad was already there, standing by the doorframe. His face was drawn, his eyes tired but searching, like he was looking for something more than just the morning news.

"How many more times will you keep escaping?" he asked, his voice low but heavy with meaning.

Caught off guard, I hesitated, my hand hovering over the newspaper. "No, I am not," I replied, my voice barely above a whisper. But even as I said it, I knew it wasn't true. I was escaping,escaping the pain, the guilt, the unsaid words that hung between us.

He laughed "Okay.Come,Let's go for a walk" and mom told us to come home early by listening to it.We went to the playground for a walk.

Dad's walk slowed. "Krish,everyone perceives their father as a hero in their childhood. But I couldn't fulfill that role for you."

I said "Dad,it's nothing like that".

"Krish, financial issues are not the only reason that I stopped you from cricket.As parents, if there is any problem at home, what we fear is your future," Dad explained earnestly, his concern for my well-being evident in his words.

"I know dad.I know that.For now, I am happy that you are beside me.Don't think about all those dad,"I replied.He patted me on my head and sat on the bench where I and Vaishnavi used to.

I sat beside him, feeling the weight of unspoken words between us. "Dad, why weren't you surprised when you saw me? You smiled right away. I've always been so cold with you, never giving you the respect you deserve."

He looked at me, his eyes softening with a warmth I hadn't seen in years. "You don't know what you did, Krish. When I see a smile on your face after such a long time, how could my fear of death not fade away? I hadn't been the 'me' I once was, but that day in the hospital, I felt reborn as happiness in you."

His words hung in the air, heavy with a truth I hadn't been ready to hear. "How? How is it possible to love someone so deeply, Dad?" I asked, my voice trembling with the weight of emotions that had been buried for too long.

He took a deep breath, his gaze never leaving mine. "I learned it from you, Krish. You suffered like hell when you lost her. How could you love someone that much, Krish?" he asked, his voice breaking as he threw the question back at me. It wasn't just a question; it was a mirror, reflecting the depth of his own love that I had never truly seen.

After Dad said those words, everything else seemed to fade away. The world grew quiet except for the gentle rustling of the wind around us. I looked at my father, and for the first time in what felt like forever, I truly saw him. Tears filled my eyes, spilling over as I tried to speak, but all I could do was nod. My reply came through those tears, a silent understanding between us.

"Okay, come. Let's go home," he said softly, wiping my tears with a tenderness that felt like home itself. In that simple gesture, I realized something profound: no matter how deep the hurt, no matter how lost I felt, a conversation with Mom and Dad could always bring me back. Their presence was the anchor I had overlooked for so long.

With this newfound clarity, I began preparing for my pre-final exams. Every morning, Dad would wake me up at 5 a.m., his footsteps soft yet resolute, a reminder of his steadfast care. He'd bring me a cup of tea, its aroma filling the air before his voice did. Somehow, Dad's tea tasted better than Mom's,the smell alone was enough to stir me from sleep.

As always, Subinay and I used to go to school together.Studying for the exams without her was a bit difficult for both of us.

"There will be pain, Krish, but if we put that pain on our education, it will not make sense."Subinay said when we were studying.Without thinking about all this, I did well in my exams.

As soon as I returned home after my final exam, I found Dad waiting on the balcony. "Krish, we're going out tomorrow. Pack your bags for two days," he said.

Where are we going,dad?

"Deva",dad replied. Dad looked at mom and said "He asked us to visit."

Mom nodded. "Dad,but he will.." Chitra tried to stop us from going.Everyone were looking at me.

"I will be fine,Mom.Let us go"

Dad put his hands on my shoulders "I will be with Krish, right? Don't worry."Mom agreed.She asked us to have dinner and sleep earlier.We needed to take the first bus.

To be honest,I didn't sleep much that night. Chitra looked at me "What are you thinking?"

"I am scared, Chitra".

"Why?"She asked.

"I don't know either.When dad said that we will meet them tomorrow,look,exactly here, I am feeling something" I pointed my heart to her.

"I think you know what you are feeling,Krish" she replied. She turned the lights on and sat behind me "You are scared that if her father says to forget Vaishnavi Or if you go, this will be your last memory of her. Isn't it? You don't want to hear those words from him because you listen to him."

She was right. I actually listen to him. Mr.Deva and I have to comfort each other. If I am happy, so are they.

"You need to be strong, Okay? Now, go to bed" Chitra comforted me.After waking up, we got ready and hopped on the first bus to bangalore.

We landed in Bangalore,Dad booked a taxi to the village where Vaishnavi's parents are living.While we were going "Take that left route" Dad said to the driver.

"Sir,but that is.." the driver was going to say something.

"I know.Just go,"Dad replied.

After some time, the car came to a halt, and there was nobody in sight.Dad got out of the car and told me to do the same.I opened the car door and looked around, it was a graveyard.

There was her grave.Vaishnavi's.

"Sorry I slept, tell me now, How is the night sky,Krish?" Vaishnavi asked me.She looked at my eyes "Are you crying?".

"No.I am happy",I replied by wiping my tears.

"Okay.You know what, my grandma said that those who have passed on will stay in the stars, observing their loved ones from above."

"Really?"I was surprised.

"Yes,really. So If I am gone, you don't need to go to my grave to see me.Even if you do, let it be your last time.Look up, I will be watching you from there" she said, gently turning my face towards the sky.

"Stop it, why are you talking about it now?" I asked aloud in anger.

"Keep your cool,Kiddo",she teased.

I crumpled to the ground, wailing loudly.The driver came to wake me up "Sir, your son."

"Let him," Dad said.

"They are waiting for us,Krish.We need to go.Get up" dad asked me after a while.I ignored and stayed at her grave.

"How long will you stay there, she will not come again" someone shouted from behind.I know who it was, it's Mr.Deva.

I turned back, he came close to me "I can't even ask you how you are.What is that crying? Seeing you like that makes me feel scared."

"Are you happy? I can imagine how you are feeling.Not only you, I'm also scared to see you like this.I can see the weight of tears that your eyes are carrying, they are waiting to come out." I said aloud by looking at his eyes.

He swiftly pulled me close and hugged me tightly. "Alright, let's head home, Krish," Mr.Deva said, leading the way.

"Let's go, Mr.Vyas" Uncle told dad.

Dad opened the car door, quickly gathered some flowers, and hurried to her grave to place them there.While he was placing the flowers there, Uncle said "Your father writes letters to us every month, he keeps checking on us."

"What?Letters?He really did?" I exclaimed.

"Yes. Letters.Your father is not old fashioned, but an innocent who is not used to the new generation.Otherwise, he does not like the new generation,"Uncle replied.

Krish,everyone perceives their father as a hero in their childhood. But I couldn't fulfill that role for you.

"You are,dad.You are."

Dad asked me to stay at Mr.Deva's home for 2 days. I held his hand "stay with me,dad."

"I would love to, but your mom and sister are there ,right? I should go,"dad said.

"Okay,"I replied.

Uncle and I started from the Graveyard to his home and dad left for the bus station.Mrs.Deva was waiting for us at the home.As soon as I saw her,I embraced her.

"How are you, dear?"She asked.

I nodded "I am good". She made my favorite breakfast 'Dosa with ground nut chutney'. After we had breakfast, we just spent some time together.We had a great time with each other.

"Krish, We are trying to move on and you should too" Mrs.Deva said.I couldn't tell them anything except that I would try.

"Go and take some rest,Krish. We will go to a restaurant for lunch",Mr.Deva said.When I went to bed, the room was full of her books and photos.I sat on the bed and I was looking at them.

"Why are you not sleeping, dear?"Mrs.Deva came to me.She went to Vaishnavi's photo frame "This is her childhood photo, when she was 6 years old."

"She is cute," I replied with a smile.

"That is her last pic which we happily took.Since then, every photo we've taken has been meant to hold onto her memories."She said.

"Don't ever think you don't have any children,mom," I said, wiping her tears.When she heard me call out 'Mom' she drew near to me, placing her hand on my head and she said, "God bless you"

She told me to go to bed and left.This time I fell asleep.After I slept for a while, uncle came "Hey champ,time to wake up."

"Huh?" I replied, rubbing my eyes.He reminded me of the lunch plan at the restaurant.We started our journey from home at 2 o'clock.

After reaching the restaurant, we eagerly entered and indulged in a delightful lunch, savoring each flavorful bite and relishing the company of one another. We decided to extend our outing by heading to a nearby park. We were walking and enjoying nature there.

Mr.Deva asked "So, when are your final exams?".I sighed, checking the time table on my phone. "They start next Monday with math, then it's history on Tuesday, followed by science on Wednesday. It's going to be a busy week!" I replied.

"Remember,Krish,prepare well," Mr.Deva said.Mrs.Deva was trying to convince him that I'll do well on exams.I was confused to say anything.Its not like I feel depressed but whenever I am smiling and I am happy, I get a feeling like I should not be happy.

"My heart is not remembering me without her,I am trying to force it but it is causing me pain."I replied.They both stood in front me,Mrs.Deva said "You will get through that phase,Krish".I nodded.

"I will go and get ice cream for us.Krish,Do you like blackcurrant?"Mrs.Deva asked me.

"I love it."

When she left to get ice cream, Mr.Deva looked at me "Krish,you are going to college in a few months,right after your final exams.School life is a dream, after that you go to reality.That's why everyone likes school life,no one likes the reality.You need to be careful with people,Study well, Okay?"

"Sure,Mr.Deva,I Promise,"I replied.He was trying to tell me something.I asked if there was anything else he was trying to say.

After knowing about her condition, she would often remark, "It's amazing how much joy we experience when we share someone's pain or make them happy during their tough times.So Krish, If you see someone who is really fighting to live,don't miss the opportunity to make them happy"he shared Vaishnavi's words.

I had chills when he said that to me.It seemed real.Those words resonated deeply within me.Mrs.Deva bought ice cream,we left after a few minutes.Leaving the park, Mr.Deva and I strolled down the winding path, our laughter mingling with the fading echoes of children's voices.

"Mrs. Deva, that ice cream was amazing!"I said, excitement evident in my voice.

Mrs. Deva chuckled. "You're welcome, kiddo! I'm glad you enjoyed it. Do you have a favorite flavor?".

"Definitely the blackcurrant! It was so delicious," I replied eagerly. "What about you, Mr.Deva?"

"I'm a classic vanilla kind of guy myself," Mr.Deva admitted with a grin. "Can't go wrong with the classics, right?"

"Yeah, vanilla's good too,"I agreed.

Mrs. Deva whispered in my ear, "He doesn't have good taste" and we were laughing behind him.It was such a fun day in the park."Now, let's go make some dinner together when we get home."Mr.Deva cheered us like a kid.

"Yeah.Let's do it," I and Mrs.Deva extended the cheering.We reached home, the familiar comfort enveloping us as we stepped through the door.I exchanged a smile with Mr.Deva, silently thanking him once again for the wonderful afternoon.

With anticipation for the evening ahead, I eagerly followed him into the kitchen, ready to lend a hand and make more memories together as a family.

"Mr.Deva, can we have dinner on the terrace?" I asked him.Mr.Deva paused, considering my request with a thoughtful expression. After a moment, he smiled and nodded. "Sure thing, Krish. Dinner on the terrace sounds like a wonderful idea."

He knew that I remembered the day when we had dinner last time together.

As we made our way to the terrace, the setting sun painted the sky in hues of orange and pink, casting a warm glow over everything it touched. We set the table and took our seats.

"This is perfect," I said, enjoying the peaceful setting.We savored our meal in the serenity of the evening, the laughter and conversation flowing freely between us.I couldn't help but feel grateful for moments like these, shared with loved ones amidst the beauty of nature.We decided to sleep on the terrace.

"Vaishnavi and I love the night sky so much," I said, my gaze fixed on the twinkling stars above.Mr.Deva nodded, his expression tinged with sadness.

"She told me that we find peace when we look at the night sky," I shared softly, my gaze drifting upward once more.Mr.Deva's eyes softened as he looked up at the stars with me.

Mrs.Deva placed a comforting hand on my shoulder.I held her hand and said "I can feel her presence among the stars."

As we stood together beneath the silent canopy of the night, I felt a sense of unity with them, bound by our shared memories and the enduring love we held for Vaishnavi.

We settled down on the terrace, the cool night air wrapping around us like a comforting blanket. With the gentle rustle of leaves and the distant hum of crickets, we drifted off into a peaceful slumber beneath the watchful gaze of the stars.

I woke up on the terrace, the morning sun gently caressing my face. I found Mr.Deva and Mrs.Deva already awake, sitting nearby and savoring their morning tea. "Good morning, Krish," Mr.Deva greeted with a warm smile. "Did you sleep well?"

"Good morning," I replied with a stretch, feeling refreshed from the night's rest. "Yes,I need to catch the 11 AM bus back home."

Mrs.Deva nodded understandingly. "Of course, dear. We'll help you get ready." She then added with a gentle smile, "Come,Have your tea first."

Sitting down with them, I savored the warm tea.When I was packing everything, "Mr.Deva, Can I have Vaishnavi's collection of novels? I think I should start reading novels,"I asked.

Mr.Deva agreed, his eyes lighting up with encouragement. "Of Course, Krish," he replied gently. "They're in her room. You can go and collect them"

As I prepared to leave, Mrs.Deva approached me with a warm smile, her eyes soft with affection. "Take care, Krish," she said softly, squeezing my hand gently. "Remember, you're always welcome here."

Her words conveyed a sense of genuine affection, and I felt a pang of sadness knowing that I would be missed. "Thank you, Mom," I replied with a heartfelt hug and a whispered goodbye.

Mr.Deva stood by my side, ready to accompany me to the bus station. With a final wave to Mrs.Deva, I followed Mr.Deva out of the door.

Mr.Deva and I arrived at the bus station. "I'll definitely do well in my exams.I am grateful for your kindness and support, I knew that even as I left your home, you and Mrs.Deva love would continue to guide me on my path.I miss you,"With those words, I hugged him tightly.

Mr.Deva returned the hug warmly, his eyes reflecting a sense of pride and warmth. "You'll do great, Krish," he said with a reassuring smile. "Remember, we're always here for you, no matter where life takes you."

When the bus arrived, I exchanged one last embrace with Mr.Deva before stepping aboard. With a bittersweet smile, I found a seat by the window and watched as Mr.Deva's figure grew smaller in the distance. With a heavy heart, I raised my hand and waved goodbye.

7
In the wake of words

With a sigh of relief, I closed my final exam booklet, marking the end of weeks filled with late-night study sessions and endless cramming. As I handed in my papers, a wave of mixed emotions washed over me—relief that the ordeal was finally over, yet a nagging worry lingered about how I had performed, especially in math, my Achilles' heel.

Walking out of the exam hall, I caught a glimpse of my dad waiting anxiously by the gate, his eyes scanning the crowd for my familiar face. Relief flooded his expression as he spotted me, a proud smile spreading across his face.

I couldn't help but feel a twinge of guilt as I approached him, knowing that my performance in math might not meet his high expectations.

"Dad, I'm done," I announced, trying to sound confident despite the gnawing uncertainty in my gut.

He enveloped me in a tight hug, his pride palpable in the way he held me close. "I'm proud of you, son," he said, his voice tinged with genuine admiration. "You worked hard, and that's what matters the most."

As we made our way home, my mind buzzed with thoughts of what the future held. Despite my less-than-stellar performance in math, I found solace in the knowledge that I had excelled in my other subjects.

"So, have you thought about which college you want to join?"Dad inquired.I shrugged, feeling a mixture of excitement and apprehension about the next step in my academic journey. "Not really, Dad. I've been thinking about it, but I'm not sure yet."

"Well, take your time. We'll figure it out together,"Dad said reassuringly.

While Dad readied himself to leave, I hesitated before mustering the courage to ask, "Dad, would you be okay if I enrolled in a college that's far away?".

"Of course, I would," he replied without hesitation. "I understand your concern, but don't worry about the expenses.Our issues with Sravanth's debt were cleared,".During my intermediate, I immersed myself in the world of literature, devouring novels that transported me to different realms. Alongside my literary journey, I developed a deep appreciation for the art of Vincent van Gogh, losing myself in the vibrant colors and emotional depth of his masterpieces. This period was a fusion of words and art, each enriching my understanding and love for creativity in its myriad forms.

I loved the feeling of losing myself in the lives of the characters, as if I were experiencing their adventures and emotions firsthand. With each turn of the page, I found myself drawn deeper into their worlds.That's how my love for words grew.

I made a simple yet significant purchase—a small notebook, its pristine pages eagerly awaiting the ink of my thoughts and reflections. With pen in hand, I sat at my desk, the faint glow of the lamp casting a warm, inviting light as I prepared to pour out my innermost thoughts onto the blank canvas of the page.

"Vyas,Turn off the lights and sleep!" Mom's voice rang out.

I glanced up, momentarily confused. Was Dad already home? I called out, "Dad?".

Dad appeared in the doorway, his figure outlined by the dim light filtering in from the hall. "I'm here, it's not me," he said softly.

As Chitra stepped into the room, her expressions shifted from confusion to surprise as she laid eyes on me, sitting at dad's desk with the diary open before me.

"What? Are you writing a diary?Seriously?" She was shocked "Mom,It's not dad".Dad entered the room,with a smile playing at the corners of his lips."Hey there, deep in thought?" Dad asked.

"I'm not really into books and diaries but I am just writing my thoughts dad," I admitted.He knew that I hated books and diaries.

"But,Vaishnavi changed me.Unintentionally, she sparked my love for words.She showed me the values in them.So,as long as I live, every word I write is dedicated to her," I said.

"I'm genuinely happy for you, Krish," Dad expressed.I wrote a few lines and I shared it with them.

It goes like :

Am I suffering from talking to people I like?

Or,am I just talking to them even though I know I'll suffer?

Do I suffer to be liked?

Or, I Love to suffer?

Will the answer be in my teary eyes?

Or is it in the eyes that I love?

Eyes that I seek,should not be the cause of my tears

And

My tears should not wet their eyes.

"That's incredible, Krish,"Dad remarked, his hand gently resting on my shoulder in support.Mom gave me the blanket "Get some rest, okay? Sleep in this room after you finish it."

"Goodnight, Krish," They said, before turning to leave the room.Alone in the quiet of the room, I returned to my writing.

Days went by, I focused on preparing for the EAMCET exam.Hours of studying, countless practice tests, and unwavering focus culminated in a moment of success when the results were announced—I and Subinay had secured a seat in Hyderabad.

"It's a good college," Mom said, her voice tinged with excitement.Dad nodded in agreement, a pride spreading across his face. "Absolutely, we're really happy for you, Krish."Their words filled me with a sense of satisfaction, knowing that my efforts had brought joy to my parents.

Few days later,the time approached for me to leave for college, a somber atmosphere settled over our home.When I was a kid,I could not spend a single day without my mom but now I'm leaving.

The weight of leaving home for the first time settled heavily on my chest. Mom's embrace felt like a lifeline, her arms wrapped around me as if she could shield me from the uncertainties ahead. Her whispered words "I will miss you,"carried a mixture of pride and apprehension, the warmth of her love mingling with the bittersweet taste of farewell.

I squeezed her back, fighting back my own emotions, determined to be strong for her. "I'll miss you too, Mom," I managed to say, my voice catching in my throat.

Dad tried to put on a brave face, but I could see the sadness lurking behind his smile.

Dad stepped forward, his attempt at a reassuring smile not quite reaching his eyes. His hands found their way to my shoulders, a silent gesture of support. "You've got this," he said, his voice steady despite the emotions simmering beneath the surface. "But remember, we're just a phone call away. Anytime, anywhere, no matter what."

As Subinay and I maneuvered our luggage onto the train, the weight of impending separation settled heavily upon me. My family stood on the platform, their faces a mosaic of mixed emotions—smiles masking the underlying sadness of our imminent parting.

I struggled to find the right words to convey the depth of my emotions, the ache of leaving them behind tugging at my heartstrings. Unable to articulate the torrent of feelings surging within me, I settled for silence, my gaze lingering on each familiar face, committing every detail to memory.

They understood, as they always did, the unspoken language of our shared bond, and amidst the hustle and bustle of the station, our silent exchange spoke volumes.

The train started moving, the rhythmic clack of the tracks beneath me set a somber tone. I leaned against the window, watching as my family stood on the platform, their faces filled with a mixture of pride and sadness. My mother waved frantically, her handkerchief fluttering in the wind, while my father stood tall, his stoic demeanor barely masking the emotion in his eyes.

I raised my hand in farewell, my heart heavy with the weight of leaving them behind. The train gathered speed, and their figures slowly shrank into the distance, becoming mere specks against the backdrop of the station. But even as they faded from view, I carried their love and support within me like a beacon in the night.

A lump formed in my throat, threatening to choke back the words I wanted to say.I wiped away a stray tear and whispered a silent promise to myself: no matter how far apart we were, their love would always be my guiding light, illuminating the path ahead.

We strolled through the quiet campus, the morning sun cast long shadows across the manicured lawns and ivy-covered buildings. The air was crisp and still, carrying the faint scent of dew and freshly-cut grass. A sense of anticipation hung in the air, mingled with the excitement of embarking on a new chapter of our lives.

"We're here before most people even wake up," Subinay replied with a grin.

I nodded in agreement, feeling a sense of awe wash over me at the sight of the imposing academic buildings. "Let's head to the hostel first," I suggested, eager to settle into our new surroundings.

We made our way towards the hostel, the sound of our footsteps echoed in the empty corridors. The silence was punctuated only by the occasional chirping of birds.

The receptionist welcomed us with a warm smile, handing over the keys to our rooms.

We had our rooms and it's convenient.

With backpacks slung over our shoulders and anticipation coursing through our veins, we set off towards the college campus.

"Ready for our first day of college?" I asked Subinay.His excitement matching my own "Absolutely" Subinay replied.Entering the college campus,we were greeted by a sea of unfamiliar faces.

I don't know who I will be with and who I will fight with.I aimed to be choosy with whom I befriended, preferring not to be too open with everyone.

Subinay's easygoing nature and sense of humor make him capable of striking up friendships with anyone, so it's no surprise that my benchmates are also as funny as him.

Within a few days, I made friends.Roopesh,Mahesh joined us.The two girls always enjoy themselves like kids,Priya and Seetha.

I used to hang out with our bench crew while in class.It became a habit to be with Priya and Seetha after the classes were over.

In the heart of the bustling canteen, surrounded by the clamor of voices and the clatter of trays, I spotted her for the first time. Anshu sat there, a vision of tranquil beauty amidst the chaos. Her dress, a serene shade of blue, seemed to cast a gentle glow, like a moon casting its light over a sunlit afternoon. She sat with a quiet grace, her presence a stark contrast to the lively atmosphere around her.

I couldn't tear my eyes away. Her calm demeanor was like a still pond in the middle of a storm, drawing me in with its peaceful allure. The noise of the canteen seemed to fade, leaving only the image of her serene figure etched in my mind.

Later that evening, as I sat alone in the dimly lit room, the memory of her presence lingered like a sweet, haunting melody. I found myself reaching for my notebook, compelled to translate the feelings she had stirred within me into words. With every stroke of the pen, I poured my thoughts and emotions onto the page, capturing the essence of the moment when I first saw her. Each line I wrote felt like a tribute to the quiet beauty that had so effortlessly captured my heart.

In the night's gentle glow, she smiled bright,
Even the stars envied her light.
Leaving the sky's vast blue,
Would she grace my world, too?
Could she be the moon, just for me,
Shining in my universe, endlessly free?

Subinay's curiosity sparked as he watched a faint blush creep across my cheeks. His eyes twinkled with mischief. "Ah, writing about a special someone?" he teased, his voice light and playful.

I chuckled nervously, feeling the heat rise in my face. I couldn't deny the truth, though I wished he'd let it drop. "Maybe," I admitted, hoping my hesitance would be enough to steer him away from probing further.

Subinay leaned in slightly, his smirk widening. "Thinking of starting a conversation?" he quipped, his tone dripping with knowing amusement. The teasing glint in his eyes made it clear he wasn't going to let the subject slide easily.

."Yeah, thinking about it. I'll talk to her tomorrow"I replied.The following day, I summoned the courage to approach her.My heart skipped a beat as I spotted her seated in front of our block in a color of magenta.

Subinay raised an eyebrow as he noticed me staring intently in her direction. "Feeling brave today, huh?"he asked.I nodded.

"Yeah, I think it's time," I replied.

I saw tears in her eyes, as I was going near her. "Krish, hold on. Something seems off. Look at her, she's crying" Subinay said.

"But I need to talk to her," I insisted.He shook his head firmly. "No, hold on. She's in tears. It's not the right time"

I handed him the paper I was holding. "What are you up to?" Subinay inquired.

It's amazing how much joy we experience when we share someone's pain or make them happy during their tough times.So Krish, If you see someone who is really fighting to live,don't miss the opportunity to make them happy.

Those words made me walk towards Anshu but I found myself at a loss for words.Not knowing what to say,I remembered the words that changed my life, and with those words I started my life again.

I stood in front of Anshu and uttered those words that resonated deeply within me.

"Hey Kiddo".

Epilogue

My hands felt warm.I woke up in the hospital, finding Anshu lying beside me, her hand resting in mine.I regained consciousness in the hospital after I relived my memories.

As I opened my eyes, she immediately called my parents, who were waiting just outside.Their faces were filled with relief and concern. I felt reborn.

I don't get why my reliving ended after seeing Anshu.The solution revealed itself in the rustling of papers being carried by the wind on my bed.

My Journal.I started writing a journal from the day I met Anshu.Each time I pen down my thoughts in my journal, and every subsequent reading, I relive.That's why I relived memories from before I began journaling.

That day my life breathed again and told me who I am.There are many things in our life that bring us to tears, but somehow the solution to all of them is words.Those words can be the cause of our tears, it can be the expression of love, it can be the sharing of solitude.You cannot tell which of them will give you pleasure and which will give you pain.Not only with our hands, but we can also wipe away tears with words like my dad words in his book and Vaishnavi's words in her voice.

In that moment, I realized what love,life truly was — a sensation beyond definition, untouched by poets, writers, songs, or words. And when you finally get to know what love is, you choose to love yourself.

If love is within you, it's plenty.Only then can you extend love to all things.

There are days when you think today is good, there are days when you think today could be better.If we're satisfied with today, there's no longing for tomorrow.

Our life truly begins when our memories, once burdensome, now bring a smile to our face.Looking back on my life, I realized it's been filled with tears and words.

Tears show us pain and words are a blessing to dry them away.

Dear Reader,

As you hold "My Tears & Words" in your hands, you're not just perusing pages; you're stepping into a world where emotions intertwine with the power of words.

In every stroke of the pen, in every word carefully placed, lies my devotion to the beauty of words and the profound connection we share with nature. This book is not just a collection of prose; it's a testament to the enduring bond between humanity and the written word.

I hold a firm belief that words possess a unique ability to heal, to console, and to inspire. They are more than just symbols on a page; they are vessels of emotion and carriers of our deepest truths. Like drops of rain nourishing the earth, each word in this book carries with it the essence of my soul, hoping to resonate with yours.

Sometimes, I find myself saying 'I love you' to the sky...or whispering those words to the rain as it touches the earth, feeling its rhythm like a heartbeat of the world...or telling it to the trees, knowing they stand tall, listening, rooted yet reaching for the sky. Sometimes, we speak to nature because it feels like it understands the words we don't say. It holds our whispers in its winds and our dreams in its stars. In 'My Tears & Words,' I explored these silent conversations with the world around us.

I've often found solace in the written word, as I believe many of us have. Words have a way of staying with us, etching themselves into the fabric of our being, shaping our thoughts and guiding our journeys. They are a constant companion on the winding road of life, offering comfort in times of darkness and companionship in moments of solitude.In our journey through life, one thing remains eternal: the lasting impact of someone's words, accompanying us until our last breath.

Be with those who are in pain, your words are enough.It makes them strong.There is also a chance that they forget the pain.What could be better than that?

As you embark on this literary journey, may you find echoes of your own experiences within these pages. May you discover solace, inspiration, and perhaps even a newfound appreciation for the beauty of language and the world that surrounds us.

This is one thing I want to say through this story–Words are humanity,if it heals.Words are the deity, if it gives hope and a beautiful way to live,if it is shared.Like Vaishnavi said "Words are shadows of humans Krish.It's stays with us forever".Here,I am sharing my words with you.

With heartfelt gratitude,

K Gopichand

Playlist

Songs played a key role for me to write this book.Some of them are :

Only You - Selena Gomez

If We Love Again - Yoon Sang Hyun

With You - Jimin,Ha Sung Woon

The Night We Met - Lord Huron

Hallelujah - Kim Feel

ceilings - Lizzy McAlpine

Walk Forever By My Side - Twin Shadow

Before You Go - Lewis Capaldi

Hold On - Chord Overstreet

a thousand years - Christina Perri

You Are Not Alone - Michael Jackson

Sirivennala - Mickey J.Meyer, Anurag Kulkarni

you were good to me - Jeremy Zucker, Chelsea Cutler

Love wins all - IU

Main Ishq Mein Hoon - Manan Bharadwaj

Kaun Tujhe - Palak Mucchal

Tender Loneliness - Matija Strnisa

Never Enough - Loren Allred

Have It All - Jason Mraz

Easy On Me - Adele

Winter Bear - V

What Was I Made For? - Billie Ellish

july - dyl dion

Let It Go - James Bay

Done For Me - Instrumental - Punch

It's You - Henry

Everything Has Grown - Colouring

Hello - Sohyang

One Person - Solji

Another Love - Tom Odell

Wait - M83

Never Say Never - The Fray

In Silence - Janet Suhh

Chances - Athlete

Follow Gopichand at:

- Instagram: @gopichand.author

- Drop an E-mail:gopichandwriting@gmail.com

9 7 9 8 8 9 3 6 3 6 7 2 7